Five Nights at Freddy's™

FAZBEAR FRIGHTS #6

BLACKBIRD

Five Nights at Freddy's

FAZBEAR FRIGHTS #6
BLACKBIRD

SCOTT CAWTHON
KELLY PARRA
ANDREA WAGGENER

Scholastic Inc.

Photo of TV static: © Klikk/Dreamstime

All rights reserved. Published by Scholastic Inc., *Publishers since 1920*. SCHOLASTIC and associated logos are trademarks and/or registered trademarks of Scholastic Inc.

The publisher does not have any control over and does not assume any responsibility for author or third-party websites or their content.

This book is a work of fiction. Names, characters, places, and incidents are either the product of the author's imagination or are used fictitiously, and any resemblance to actual persons, living or dead, business establishments, events, or locales is entirely coincidental.

Library of Congress Cataloging-in-Publication Data available

ISBN 978-1-338-70389-4

2 2021

Printed in the U.S.A.   23

First printing 2021 • Book design by Betsy Peterschmidt

TABLE OF CONTENTS

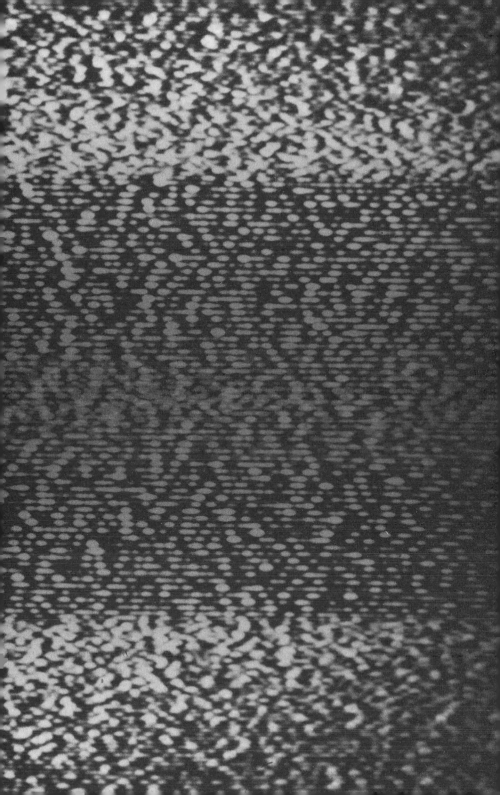

It needs to be bloody." Nole sat backward on his chair, its straight back between his splayed legs. In spite of the chair's cheap tan plastic and the rest of the room's less-than-upscale ambiance, Nole managed to look cool and confident. Sam wondered how he pulled that off so easily.

Feeling like the nerd that he was, Sam tried to adjust his long legs to fit another of the cheap plastic chairs. He disagreed with Nole: "Horror's not in the blood. It's in the creep factor."

"Creep factor," Nole repeated.

"It's a technical term."

Nole nodded. "I must've dozed off when Grimmly was talking about that."

"More likely you were staring at Darla Stewart."

"You make a point."

"And we're not getting anywhere." Sam sighed and

shifted in his seat again. His legs were cramping. He was hungry. And he was pretty sure he and Nole were the only pair in the room who hadn't come up with an idea yet.

Although Sam's back was to the rest of the space, he could hear the jumble of eight hushed conversations going on all over the gray-walled room. The classroom had little to muffle the intense babble: a few folding tables, some plastic chairs, a portable closet packed with sound equipment, and a viewing screen. Through an open door behind Nole, Sam could see the project room, which had open space for filming scenes, a green screen, and several shelves stuffed full of more AV equipment. The conversations between Sam's classmates were mostly incomprehensible because they were taking place in cautious whispers and mumbles, lest a brilliant idea get stolen. Occasionally, though, someone would get excited, and Sam could make out a word: *serial killer, zombie, vampire, demon.* The words he heard drained some of the tension from his shoulders. If those were the other teams' ideas, maybe he and Nole still had a chance. They didn't have an idea yet, but at least they didn't have a done-to-death idea.

"You have to admit she has a fine caboose," Nole said.

Sam stretched all 37 inches of his legs and stared at his huge feet. Both Sam's legs and his feet defied the normal proportions that should have gone with his six-foot-five body. According to a chart his doctor showed him once, his legs should have been about 34½ inches long. You wouldn't think 2½ extra inches would be much, but apparently they were enough to make Sam look like a stork or a heron or a crane (he'd heard all three from various unkind kids). And those inches were enough to make him prone to grand displays of ungainly clumsiness, which prevented him from turning his height into something useful like, say, on a basketball court. All Sam's legs did, as far as he could tell, was get in his way.

"Earth to Sam."

"Huh?"

"Looks like we're lagging here, dude." Nole gestured out into the room behind Sam's shoulders. Sam looked around. Four teams were leaving the room. Two were getting ready to leave. Only two other teams were still talking. Great.

Actually, it was kind of great. Sam thought better in silence. He looked at his watch. The classroom was open for another half hour. They had thirty minutes to come up with something.

"Would you get out of that chair?" Nole flung his foot out and kicked the side of Sam's seat. "You're squirming so much you remind me of my nephew when he needs to take a piss."

"I can't get comfortable."

"My heart bleeds."

"There you go with the blood again."

Nole grinned. "It's all about the blood."

"Seriously. We need to think."

"Hey!" Nole's blasé posture disappeared. He glanced over at the remaining teams. "Seriously, dude, get off the chair. Come over here." Nole exited his chair with enviable grace, and he took a couple steps to the wall behind him. Sliding down the wall, he folded his normal-length legs—perfectly proportioned for his six-foot-one height—into a meditative position. He motioned to Sam again when Sam hesitated.

So Sam gave up on the too-small chair and awkwardly put his skinny body on the floor in front of Nole. He had to admit his legs were happier.

Nole leaned forward and spoke softly. "Do you remember Freddy Fazbear's Pizza?" Nole's breath smelled like licorice.

Sam leaned away. "Sure. Why?"

Nole lowered his voice into a whisper so faint Sam had trouble understanding him. All he heard was *creepy animat.* But that was enough.

"Oh, those!" Sam felt goose bumps on his arms. He was

glad he was wearing a long-sleeve T-shirt so Sam wouldn't see how the mention of the characters affected him. "Yeah, those were creepy all right."

"Thinking about pizza gave me the idea," Nole said.

"What idea?"

Nole gazed out over the classroom again. Sam checked it, too. Only one other team was left. It was the infamous Darla, her fine caboose, and her friend Amber, who actually was the nice one of the two girls. They had their heads together and seemed to be having a whispered disagreement. They weren't paying any attention to Nole and Sam.

"My idea is to write a horror story plot around a creepy animatronic of our own," Nole whispered to Sam.

Sam, edgy from just thinking about Freddy Fazbear's animatronic characters, had to admit that was a great idea. "I like it!"

"Awesome." Nole held out a fist, and Sam bumped it.

"So what would be a good character?" Nole asked.

"You're asking me?"

"You're the genius."

Sam wasn't a genius, but he did get good grades. Some people, like Nole, who tended to be a bit of a screw-off, got those things confused.

Sam leaned back and looked at his feet again. A good animatronic character. A good animatronic character. A good animatronic . . . Sam looked at his legs. Stork, heron, crane. "How about a bird? Not a chick, obviously. Something more obviously intimidating."

"That's not bad. How about a goose?"

"A goose?" Sam repeated loudly. He laughed.

"Don't laugh. A goose attacked me when I was little. I still bear the scars."

"Seriously?"

Nole pulled up the left leg of his faded jeans. He pointed at a white scar below his knee.

"It bit you?"

"Well, no. It chased me while I was on my bike. I fell off my bike and cut my knee."

Sam laughed again. Nole dropped his pant leg.

"Sorry," Sam said. "I can see you're traumatized."

Nole stared blankly into the middle distance. "You have no idea. I probably need therapy."

"I don't think I want to do a horror film about an animatronic goose," Sam said.

"You're right. We need the creep factor. What's a creepy bird?"

"You guys win the rotten-egg prize," Amber called from across the room.

"Saving the best for last," Nole said, holding his clasped hands above his head in a victory gesture.

Amber laughed. "You're an idiot."

Darla said nothing, and the two girls left the room, talking about a poetry reading for their English class.

"She likes you," Sam said.

"She thinks I'm an idiot."

"So she likes you, *and* she knows you."

Nole kicked Sam's foot.

Sam returned to the problem. "Oh, I've got it!" He sat up and said, in a solemn ominous tone, "'Once upon a midnight dreary . . .'"

"Huh?"

"Oh, come on. You're not that much of an idiot."

"I might be."

"'Quoth the Raven,'" Sam prompted.

"Huh? Oh, wait. I know this. That poem by the scary dude. Poe. Oh. A raven."

"Yeah. Only, no, not quite. The raven, obviously, is cliché. A crow would be, too. I'm thinking of a blackbird. It has the same connotation, but blackbirds are a little smaller. They're songbirds, and we actually have more of them in our area than we do crows or ravens."

"How do you know this stuff?"

"I'm a genius, remember?"

"No. I'd forgotten, because I'm an idiot."

They both laughed.

"Okay. So we've got a creepy blackbird," Nole said. "Now what?"

"Ever had one of them stare at you?" Sam asked. "I mean, *really* stare at you?"

"There was one in the quad the other day. I was thinking about skipping Psych 201, and that bird kept looking at me, and I felt so guilty I went to class."

Sam snapped his fingers. "That's dumb, but I think you're onto something."

"What?"

"Guilt."

"Idiot here, remember? You need to spell it out."

"Our animatronic, 'the Blackbird'"—Sam gave the name finger quotes—"will get you to confess your darkest secrets, and then when you do, it comes to punish you for your sins. It never lets you off the hook, never lets you rest. We can have the Blackbird basically hound some poor dude to death."

"Will there be blood?" Nole asked.

"You're a ghoul." Sam chewed on his lower lip. "Actually, a little blood might not be bad."

"'If you prick us, do we not bleed?'"

"Wow," Sam said. "You're quoting Shakespeare? Maybe your idiot thing is all an act."

"I'll never tell."

"The Blackbird will make you tell," Sam said with a wicked laugh.

Sam and Nole finally finished plotting the movie just in time for their next class. Even though he was arguably too tall for the role, Sam thought it would be fun to play the Blackbird. Nole, who honestly didn't want to dress up like a bird, said Sam's size would make the Blackbird even scarier. That left Nole with the part of the poor beleaguered guilty guy.

"I can do pathetic," Nole said proudly later that day as they shared a pizza.

"That you can," Sam agreed.

When Nole and Sam were only halfway through their pepperoni-and-jalapeño pizza, Amber came into the brick-walled restaurant and spotted them. "Do you have room for one more?" She pointed at the black vinyl booth seat Nole sat on.

Nole scooted over. "Sure. But keep your mitts off our pizza."

"I don't want your stinkin' pizza," Amber said.

Sam grinned at Amber as she flagged down a server and ordered a soda.

"So what's your movie about?" she asked.

"Wouldn't you like to know?" Nole said, eyes narrowed in suspicion.

Amber sniffed. "As if. I was just making conversation."

"What's yours about?"

"It's about knitting." Her smirk said she was feeling pretty good about her project.

"Are you serious?" Nole asked.

"Absolutely."

"Will there be blood?" Nole asked.

Sam laughed and shook his head.

"Plenty," Amber said.

Nole pointed at Sam. "See? Must have blood."

Sam ignored him.

The pizza place was crowded and noisy. Above the

smells of spicy pepperoni, sausage, and tomato sauce, the small space thrummed with the beat of classic rock coming from overhead speakers. Sam waved to a few friends, then watched Amber watch Nole.

Sam wasn't sure why Nole didn't ask Amber out. She was cute. Not Sam's type . . . the few girls he'd gone out with were taller and more serious than Amber.

But Nole? Nole liked girls he could laugh with, and girls seemed to like Nole's blue eyes, athlete's body, and scruffy blond hair.

Amber, also blonde, blue-eyed, and in good shape, looked good sitting next to Nole. She even dressed like he did, usually wearing faded jeans, white shirts, and, when the weather allowed it, leather jackets.

Sam blinked when Amber leaned across the table, blowing the paper wrapping off the end of her straw and toward his face.

"He told me your movie is about a bird. I think he's lying."

Sam smiled. "Actually, he's not."

"You mean like *The Birds*?"

Nole snorted and waved a slice of pizza around. "We're not that derivative."

"Ooh. Big word," Amber said.

Sam laughed. Actually, they *were* being a little derivative, weren't they? They were piggybacking off of Freddy Fazbear's Pizza.

The hair on the back of Sam's neck prickled. Why did that happen every time he thought of the place?

Sam pulled out his wallet and threw some cash on the table. "I need to go get started."

"On what?" Amber asked.

"We'll never tell," Nole said.

Amber smacked his arm.

Ah, Sam thought. *True love.*

Many of Sam's classmates thought it was pathetic that he lived at home, but he loved it. First, he got along great with his parents, who were supportive and fun. Second, he had way more privacy and space than he'd have in a dorm; his parents had remodeled the basement into a sprawling apartment for him with his own kitchenette, bathroom, sleeping area, and space for his film projects. And third, he liked getting away from the campus at the end of the day. He could only take so much of the constant chatter, scholastic and social angst, and the frantic pace. Besides, he had no use for partying; working on his projects was more fun than drinking and acting like a moron.

Sam's house was about two miles from the college, an easy distance to walk, which was good, since he didn't have a car. He enjoyed the walk home, too. It followed the railroad tracks that ran along the top of a steep, forested drop-off into a rocky trench and culvert that separated farmland from the college's expansive acreage. Sam liked to pretend he was an old-timey vagabond—strolling along, waiting to hop a train to travel to faraway adventures. In fact, Sam was working on a screenplay about freight hoppers, set in the mid-twentieth century. He knew it was a tough lifestyle, but it held romantic appeal for him, maybe because he'd never felt like he fit in with mainstream life.

And of course, his current project wasn't going to help with that.

Three days after Sam and Nole decided on their horror movie plot, Sam sat in the special-order desk chair his mom had gotten for him, at the huge craft table in the basement. Covering the pale blond wood table were piles and piles of long black feathers. Luckily, Sam's dad was a merchandizer who had a gift for finding rare items—he could locate pretty much anything Sam ever needed for his projects. Today, his dad had met Sam in the driveway with several crates of feathers, which he'd helped Sam transport down the basement stairs. Before leaving the basement, Sam's dad sang out, "'Bye, bye, Blackbird.'"

"Very funny, Dad," Sam called up the stairs.

He smiled at the answering chuckle and began pulling feathers from the crates.

Sam's idea for the Blackbird costume was to weave long black feathers into a netted black fabric that would then be sewn onto a black body-hugging suit, like a feathered body wrap. This was going to require a lot of feather placing, affixing, and sewing. So Sam queued up some bluesy jazz and got to work.

At 11:30 p.m., Sam startled when the phone rang. It was Nole.

"Amber asked me out."

"Good."

"I thought I was supposed to do the asking out?"

"Have you ever heard of women's lib?"

"Vaguely. But I come from a family of male chauvinists. I'm still in the learning curve."

"What did you say to her?" Sam winced, stabbing his finger with the needle for the hundredth time.

"I said yes. I couldn't think fast enough to say anything else. Besides, I've decided her caboose might be as fine as Darla's."

"That's important."

"How's the costume coming?"

"Good, I think. I should have it done by tomorrow afternoon, and we can work on the set."

"Which is a tragedy," Nole complained.

"The set?"

"No working on it tomorrow. Tomorrow's a Saturday. Saturdays are for frolicking."

"It's the only time we could get the shooting studio assigned to us," Sam reminded him.

"A pity."

Sam ignored him, hung up the phone, and returned to sewing feathers.

A few hours later, he put the finishing touches on the costume: attaching to the head two beady yellow-and-black eyes and a tiny pointed orange beak. Even though he was exhausted, he donned the suit and stood in front of the full-length mirror behind the bathroom door.

Sam nearly shrieked when he saw himself . . . because what he was looking at wasn't *him* anymore. It was so not him he was tempted to tear off the suit and find himself again. He felt like his creation had assimilated him. He'd been transformed. He couldn't see any part of Sam. All he saw was a monster-size blackbird. His design had come out just how he'd envisioned it—the oversize proportions made the suit look almost kid-friendly, but the wide, dead eyes and dripping midnight feathers were deeply unsettling. He had no doubt that poor Floyd, the character in their movie, would seriously regret his dark secrets when he came face-to-face with the Blackbird.

Thanks to the massive quantity of feathers his dad got for him, Sam had been able to approximate the full-belly shape of a blackbird. He'd fashioned the curve of the belly to come all the way down to below his knees so the bird's legs started at his shins, conveying realistic proportions. His mom had helped him with the feet part of the costume. His mom, who loved all things crafty, found a pair of stretch-to-fit water shoes and extra-extra-large black tights with a scales pattern. She also showed Sam how to shape the bird toes out of black rubber, into which he then carved deep grooves. Together, they used sculpting epoxy to create bird claws, which Sam inserted into the rubber toes. He attached the bird feet to the water shoes so it looked like the toes extended out naturally.

At first glance, Sam was a huge blackbird. And he was beyond creepy. Now they just needed a little blood.

Sam laughed. Maybe then Nole would shut up about the blood.

Nole and Sam met Saturday afternoon to design their movie set. Nole would rather have been playing volleyball with his fraternity brothers, but in spite of his nonchalant posturing, film class mattered to him. Plus, he was stoked about their movie.

When Nole arrived in the shooting studio, Sam immediately showed him a picture of the Blackbird suit. Nole was glad Sam wasn't looking at him when Nole first saw the picture. He was pretty sure he went pale. It felt like he'd gone pale. He'd suddenly gotten cold and weak and shaky. What the heck was happening?

When Sam turned to ask Nole what he thought, Nole bent over and pretended to tie his shoe. "It's rad. Above and beyond, dude."

"Yeah? Thanks. I kind of freaked myself out when I looked in the mirror," Sam said.

Nole rose, pretty sure his normal coloring was back. Leave it to Sam to admit that he was freaked out. Sam had no clue how to be cool. He was too honest, too open, and too himself to get within sniffing distance of cool.

"Okay, so we're thinking bedroom, right?" Sam stood in the middle of the set.

"Nightmares. Night terrors. Cold sweats. Paranoid self-defense. Panicked phone calls. Yep. I think it's the ultimate in a film for a one-room set." Nole pretended to speak into a megaphone. "Step right up, folks. Get all your creep factor right here. One-stop shopping."

Sam laughed.

Nole grinned.

Sam wasn't bad-looking when he laughed, Nole thought. Sam's problem was that he always looked so serious. With strong features, a wide mouth, and a sharp jawline, Sam usually came across as harsh and angry even when he wasn't. His face was like one of those carvings on totem poles. In fact, when Nole had met Sam at the beginning of the semester the previous year, he'd asked Sam if he *was* a totem pole. The dude was *so* tall, and he wore a lot of black, red, and tan.

"Do I have something on my face?" Sam asked.

"Just your ugly mug." Nole gave Sam a playful punch to let Sam know he was kidding.

"Come on, man." Sam tossed Nole a screwdriver. "Let's get to work."

Over the next two hours, they built furniture, hung pictures, made the bed, and argued about which personal and decor items went where and why. Sam seemed to have a particularly entrenched opinion about dirty socks.

"This movie is about airing your dirty laundry and what happens to you when you do. The dirty socks should have a prominent place in the visual narrative, not just be tossed off to the side," Sam said.

Nole held up his hands. "I give."

After another half hour, Nole was getting bored. "So,

Sam, what dark secrets could the Blackbird get out of you?"

Sam dropped the stack of magazines he was carrying.

Nole laughed. "Guilt much?"

Sam shook his head. "Coincidence."

"Uh-huh." Nole looked at Sam. "Well?"

"I don't have any dark secrets," Sam said.

The way he industriously cleaned up the magazines made Nole think Sam was hiding something. "Come on, dude, spill." Nole laughed. "The secrets, not the magazines."

Sam finished restacking the magazines, and he straightened. He looked down at Nole. "Nothing to spill. What about you?"

Sam really is a nerd, Nole thought. He wasn't the kind of guy Nole usually hung out with, but Sam was a genius in film class. *Always hitch your wagon to the best horse*, Nole's grandfather used to say. Nole's grandfather was a multimillionaire. Nole figured taking his grandfather's advice was pretty wise.

"Okay," Nole conceded. "I'll tell you mine." He threw himself on the bed and put his hands behind his head.

"Hey," Sam said. "Shoes. I borrowed that bedspread."

"Fine, *Mom*." Nole kicked off his shoes.

Sam ignored him and started hanging curtains over a fake window.

"So, I'm not proud of this," Nole said.

But was that true? Might it be possible, if he was really

telling the truth about his dark secret, that he *was* a little proud of it?

"If it's a dark secret, I don't know why you would be proud of it," Sam said.

"Okay. Whatever. So when I was in junior high—I would've been maybe twelve or so, I guess . . . I was a bully."

Sam turned around and gave Nole a long look. "What do you mean?" Sam asked.

"You know, a *bully*." Nole chuckled. "A pretty ruthless bully, actually."

"Give me an example," Sam said.

What was wrong with Sam's voice? It sounded stiff.

Nole looked up at the ceiling and thought back. "Well, you know, the usual. Basically, I called 'em as I saw 'em."

Sam leaned against the wall and stared at Nole. "I still don't get it."

Nole sat up in the bed. "Okay, so there was this really awkward fat girl. She had all these weirdo habits, like she wouldn't look you in the eye, and she was always squeezing her hands together, and she had trouble talking. She didn't stutter, but she seemed to have trouble figuring out how to talk. She was just weird. She had funny facial expressions. And she wore the stupidest clothes I've ever seen. I mean, it looked like she did all her shopping at thrift stores, not the cool ones. Her clothes never matched and stuff. So I started calling her Second Hand, SH for short, and when she'd walk down the hall, I'd go, 'Shhhhh.' It caught on, and pretty soon everyone was doing it." Nole laughed. "That was a riot. Stuff like that. Oh, and then one time she came to school wearing these high-water pants. I mean, she looked so stupid. So my friends and I threw water in her face. Get it. High water." Nole laughed. "And she wore these thick glasses and always looked like she was squinting to find her way. So I put a dead mole in her locker and asked her if she was grieving her best friend." Nole guffawed. Sometimes he just cracked himself up.

He looked at Sam. Sam wasn't laughing.

Sam pulled out the chair they'd placed in front of the desk in Floyd's room. "You really think that stuff is funny?" Sam asked.

"Well, yeah," Nole said. "Don't you? You have to admit it's clever stuff, right? Like there was this time, I got like a bucketful of burrs . . . that took a while to do, too. It's not easy gathering burrs. But, see, the girl's name was Christine Wilber. I remember her name because of the 'burr' thing. And she had this long, stringy hair she never washed enough. So I figured I'd do burrs for Christine Wilber. Get it? *Burrs* for Wil*ber*. It was actually an experiment. I wanted to see if burrs would stick to greasy hair. Of course, I had to have a control, so when I threw the burrs, I also threw them at her friend, Valerie. Valerie had frizzy hair that I was pretty sure she washed *too much*. And sure enough, the burrs stuck better on Valerie than they did on Christine. I'll never forget them standing there outside the school like a couple monkeys picking lice off each other, trying to get those burrs out of their hair. Now, that was funny." Nole laughed.

Sam shook his head. "That's not funny."

Nole raised an eyebrow but didn't stop laughing. "Seriously? Picture it. They're like two little monkeys." He pretended to be a monkey picking lice off another monkey.

Sam frowned, stood up, and started pacing around the fake room.

Nole leaned back on the bed again. He pulled out a pillow from under the bedspread and plumped it up.

"I just made that bed," Sam snapped.

"Chill. I'll fix it when I get up."

Sam kept pacing. Then he abruptly stopped. "Unless you're blind, you have to have noticed I'm not a normal-looking guy, right?"

Nole tilted his head. "You're tall, but so are a lot of my frat brothers."

"They're tall and athletic," Sam said. "I'm just tall."

"Okay."

"So when I was in junior high, I was already way too tall for my age, and my legs looked even longer than they do now because I was so skinny. So guess what happened to me."

Nole figured Sam was bullied, but he decided to wait and let Sam tell his story. Nole knew he could be an idiot, but he wasn't stupid.

"I was bullied basically from the time I entered first grade until I got to my freshman year in high school.

Then that year . . . well, that year, it stopped. But I can tell you that those jokes you think are so funny, they're not funny to the people on the receiving end of them." Sam crossed his arms and glared at Nole.

Nole laughed. "Dude, you so look like a totem pole right now. Or no, you look like one of those wooden Indian statues." Nole sat up, crossed his arms, and intoned, "How." Nole fell back on the bed and laughed.

Sam shook his head and turned around. "And that's offensive. Let's just get this done, huh?"

Nole got off the bed. Still grinning, he remade the bed, maybe not as neatly as Sam had done it, but it was made, and who said Floyd was compulsive about his bed anyway?

"Are you okay, dude?" Nole asked. Sam was keeping his back to Nole.

"I'm good." Sam turned around and surveyed the room, not looking at Nole. "I think we're done here. How about if we call it good for now, and I'll bring my costume from home tomorrow so we can start filming?"

"You don't want to run through the lines now?"

"You're the one who has lines. I thought you said you already knew them."

"I do."

"Well, then I'd say we're done." Sam stepped over to the bed and fixed Nole's messy bed-making job.

"Okay, kemosabe." Nole chuckled.

Sam flicked Nole a look, said, "See you tomorrow," and strode out of the shooting studio.

"I might have gotten on one of that dude's big ol' nerves," Nole said to himself.

Then he chuckled again. He did crack himself up.

Returning from his date that evening with Amber, Nole sauntered down the hall to his single room in the frat house, bopping his head in time to the music that vibrated the walls. The speakers were on the first floor, and this was the third, but his frat brothers were partying hard tonight. The whole house shook. It also smelled like beer, knockwurst, and unwashed laundry. He wrinkled his nose. Nole didn't mind the noise, but he didn't love the smell.

Nole wouldn't have admitted it to anyone, but he wasn't really fraternity material. He'd pledged this frat because his dad and granddad had been members, and it had been assumed he'd be one, too. But it was a cool frat, and Nole was all about doing what it took to be cool. So he was content, especially since he'd won the room lottery at the beginning of the year, which got him the best single room in the three-story Tudor mansion that housed the frat.

The door Nole was strolling past flew open, and a muscular, rumpled guy with spiky black hair scratched his bare belly and squinted up at the bright hall lights. "What time is it?" he asked.

"Almost midnight," Nole said. "You okay, Ian?"

Ian was a football player, a dedicated one. He was always talking about treating his body as a temple and stuff like that.

He liked to walk around in his boxer shorts showing everyone just what an awesome temple it was. Nole thought Ian was a little full of himself, but he did find the guy's boxer shorts amusing. He had dozens of them, all in different colors and patterns. Tonight's boxers were white, but they were covered in bright yellow rubber ducks. Maybe it was the rubber ducks that made Nole notice Ian's gray claylike complexion and the dark smudges under his eyes. You don't expect someone wearing rubber ducks to look like they're terminally ill.

"Not sleeping lately. And now this." Ian waved a hand at the throbbing beat that still massaged the walls of the building.

"The music keeps you awake?"

"Yeah. Doesn't it keep you awake?"

"Nah. Nothing keeps me awake."

"Seriously?"

"Seriously. I can sleep through pretty much anything."

"I'm envious. I have trouble sleeping every night."

"Must have a guilty conscious," Nole said.

Ian's eyes widened. "Wha—?"

"Chill. Just kidding." Nole laughed and punched Ian on the cement he called an upper arm.

Ian gave Nole a weak smile and stumbled across the hall to the bathroom. Nole rubbed his knuckles and headed down the hall to his room.

Nole arrived back at the shooting studio at noon the next day, even though it was a Sunday and he generally spent his

Sundays watching sports on TV or playing intramural ball with his frat brothers. He figured he should get to the studio on time to mend things with Sam. Even though Sam hadn't said much, he was clearly pretty upset the day before. Nole might have pushed a little too far. He knew he sometimes did that.

When Nole discovered Sam wasn't in the studio yet, he stretched out on the bed to wait. Forty-five minutes later, he was still lying there. He closed his eyes and must have fallen asleep, because when Amber charged in the room he was so startled he almost fell out of the bed.

"Did you hear?"

"Huh?" He sat up. "Hear what?" He rubbed his face. "What time is it?"

"It's two thirty. The news about Sam."

"What news about Sam?"

Amber hugged herself. "They think he might have been hit by a train." She brushed at her puffy eyes.

"What?!"

"Apparently he made a costume for your movie, one with black feathers? And they found feathers all over the tracks, for like two miles. All over the place."

Nole shot off the bed. "Is he okay?"

Amber shook her head. "That's the thing. They don't know. He's missing."

"I've gotta go." Nole charged past Amber and tore out of the film studies building.

★ ★ ★

The railroad tracks ran along the back side of the campus, behind the cafeteria, rec center, and swimming pool complex. They were about a half mile from the film studies building. Jogging past kids throwing Frisbee in the quad and others studying in the shade of the campus's big cedar trees, Nole ignored several greetings and concentrated on getting to the tracks.

Hit by a train? Missing? Nole couldn't believe it. When Nole reached the tracks, his stomach clenched at the sight of a half dozen cop cars pulled up alongside the tracks and double that number of cops walking the area, their gazes to the ground. Pushing into the relatively docile crowd hanging out behind crime scene tape guarded by a large, balding cop, Nole approached the cop and said, "I'm Sam's friend. Have you found him yet?"

"*Who* are you?" the cop asked.

"Sam's friend," Nole repeated. "Nole Markham." Nole saw no reason to keep his name a secret. He hadn't done anything wrong. Had he?

"You know something about what happened here?" the cop asked.

"I only know what a friend told me, that because of the feathers, you think Sam was hit by a train and you can't find him."

The cop eyed him.

Could the guy have been more of a cliché? Big gut, shiny head surrounded by a black fringe of hair, dark eyes squinted to try and intimidate Nole, thick hands resting on his gun belt—the cop could have walked off a TV set. Except this cop smelled like hair gel and cheap cologne. At least TV cops were unscented.

Nole eyed the cop right back.

"If you don't have something to tell us," the cop said, toying with his nightstick, "get back there with everyone else."

Nole didn't move. He leaned to his right to see past the cop. Even from here, he could see black feathers fluttering over the tracks. The cop shifted his stance, and that's when Nole noticed the tall couple standing between one of the police cars and a bright red Chevy Suburban. They were talking with a guy in a baggy suit.

Nole bit the inside of his cheek so he wouldn't groan out loud. Those were Sam's parents, Paul and Molly O'Neil. He'd met them when they threw a party to celebrate the previous semester's completed film projects. Really nice people. Both were tall and dark like Sam, although Sam's mom wasn't *as* tall. She was almost as tall as Nole, though. Hefty, too. If there was something called Mom league in the NFL, she could have played. "Call me Molly," she'd said when Nole had met her. "Mrs. O'Neil is my mother-in-law." Nole remembered Molly had a great smile and an even better laugh.

Right now, she wasn't laughing. She was crying, her head pressed against her husband's shoulder. Nole clenched his fists in frustration. How could he help?

Molly looked up, and she spotted Nole. "Nole? Is that you?"

The cop standing with Sam's parents motioned for the TV cop to let Nole past. Nole couldn't stop himself from giving the cop a smirk as he went past. But his smirk died a quick death when he saw Molly's pinched white face.

She rushed to Nole and threw her arms around him. "You heard? Oh, Nole, he's missing, but they say he probably couldn't have survived—" Her voice broke, and she turned back toward Paul.

Paul held Molly with one arm and offered his other hand for Nole to shake. Holding Molly close, Paul said, "Because of the way the feathers of his costume are scattered, they think he was probably grazed by the train and then thrown clear, but they haven't found him."

Nole frowned and watched a black feather scuttle over the ground near the rails. That's when he noticed blood on the rail, on the opposite side of the tracks. Not a lot of blood. Just one smear. But it was a big smear. A police officer was taking a picture of it.

Blood, Nole thought. *There had to be blood*, he kept telling Sam.

Nole lingered by the tracks with Sam's distraught parents the rest of the afternoon. By then, the police had declared Sam missing, presumed dead. Multiple search parties had been sent out. Nole had even been part of one. But no one found anything.

When Nole left the tracks to return to his room, he let

Molly and Paul hug him, even though he didn't want to be hugged. Being near them was like standing next to a loud-speaker for emotions; their grief was amplified by their facial expressions and memories about Sam. The clamor-ous sense of loss was more than Nole could handle. He couldn't stand to be around Molly and the cops anymore. He had to get away.

Once Nole started walking away from the scene at the tracks, he couldn't stop. He just couldn't process what had happened. How could Sam be dead?

Was it my fault?

What? Why'd he think that? He didn't do anything.

But that isn't true, is it?

He kind of did do something. He'd been a bit of a jackass the day before, and Sam had been upset. He'd tried to hide it, but Nole could tell Sam was pissed when he left the studio. So what if being upset had made him careless?

But it happened this morning, not last night, he told himself. Sam wouldn't have still been upset this morning, right?

Nole wasn't convincing himself. Why did he have to be such a jerk sometimes?

"Yo, Nole, go long!"

Nole looked up to see one of his intramural buddies holding a football and pointing. Nole dutifully trotted in the direction indicated, and caught a somewhat wobbly spiral after juggling it a couple times. He was about to throw it back, intending to return it in an upstaging per-fect spiral, but his gaze, as he brought his arm forward, landed on a large black shape just at the edge of the trees. Nole let go of the ball, and it flopped all over the place before landing fifty feet short of its target.

"Wuss," Nole's friend called.

Nole ignored him.

What had he just seen?

Nole continued to ignore his friend, who was now shouting denigrating comments about Nole's throwing abil-ity. Nole hadn't seen what he thought he'd seen, had he?

When Nole reached the trees, he looked up into the sagging branches and then down into the tangled under-brush. He saw nothing out of the ordinary. It must have been his imagination. All that talk of black feathers and Sam's costume. It was messing with his head.

A little after six, Nole's stomach came unclenched enough to remind him that he hadn't eaten since before he'd gone to the shooting studio. He needed food.

So he headed to the cafeteria. Not much of what was served there could be called "food," but he was hungry enough to eat pretty much anything at this point.

The cafeteria was only half-full, as was usual on Sundays. A lot of students went away for the weekends, and even more ate out. Usually only the nerds were around about now.

"Hey."

Nole didn't have to turn to identify the speaker. It was

Amber. He wasn't sure what to say to her—their last exchange felt like years ago. She must have come looking for an update about Sam.

Nole turned. "Hey . . ."

"I, um, never see you here on Sundays."

Nole let out a sigh of relief at the slight hint of sarcasm she managed to slide into pretty much everything that came out of her mouth . . . even when sarcasm wasn't required. He wasn't sure he could talk about Sam right now.

"That's because I'm never here on Sundays."

"So you're not here now?"

"Obviously."

Amber rolled her eyes. "So is your clone going to get in line or just stand there getting in the way?"

Nole couldn't help himself. He grinned. "He'll get in line, just so he doesn't put you out."

"Nice of him."

"He's actually a pretty nice guy." Nole stepped back and motioned for Amber to go ahead of him.

"He should give you lessons." Amber winked at Nole as she passed him.

Nole followed Amber through the line, grabbing some of this and some of that. He had no idea what he was putting on his tray. He was already distracted by what had happened to Sam, plus he was trying to puzzle out what he'd seen by the trees. And now Amber was befuddling him. He'd only recently figured out he might like her, and they'd gone on their first date the night before. It had been good, but today had kind of wiped the date from his mind. *Should I have called her by now?*

"It would have been nice," Amber said.

"What?"

"You just said, 'Should I have called her by now?'"

"I did?"

"You did." She gave him a sideways glance.

That had to be evidence of his whacked-out mental state. Nole decided maybe he should stop thinking completely.

Finding himself at a big round table covered in crumbs and smeared with something red, Nole sat down. He stared at the red smear. Surely not blood. Must have been ketchup.

Why did he have blood on the brain?

Nole glanced at Amber to be sure he hadn't said that out loud. Apparently not. She was putting blue cheese dressing on a big salad.

The cafeteria was about a third full. Conversations were muted, and silverware/dish face-offs were intermittent. Outside the wall-to-wall windows, the quad was emptying. The sun was dipping behind the tops of the trees where Nole thought he'd seen—

Nothing. I saw nothing, he told himself.

Nole looked at his tray. He blinked. Somehow he'd managed to get sauerkraut, beets, mashed potatoes, three dinner rolls without butter, two dill pickles, and three kinds of pie.

"Are you pregnant?" Amber was eyeing his tray, too.

"Apparently." Nole picked up a spoon, realizing he hadn't gotten a fork. He dug into the mashed potatoes as if all was right in the world. He noticed that the cafeteria smelled like beef stew. Was that the entrée he'd missed?

Amber chewed and then put down her fork. "I'm sorry about earlier." For once, her words were free of sarcasm.

"Earlier?"

"When I told you about Sam. I shouldn't have dropped it on you the way I did."

Nole grabbed his glass and took a drink of what was in it to wash down the gluey mashed potatoes. He discovered he'd gotten sweet iced tea. He hated sweet iced tea.

"It's okay."

Amber put her hand on Nole's arm. "No, it's not. I'm sorry. I didn't realize you two were so close."

Nole shot a look at her. Was she being sarcastic again? No, judging from the little crimp between her brows, she was concerned.

"We're not that . . . ," Nole began. Then he realized that, yeah, he was pretty close to Sam. They'd started out as a complete mismatch, assigned to work with each other. Nole was rushing his fraternity. Sam lived with his parents. Nole was cool. Sam seemed to go out of his way *not* to be cool—so screamed his almost military haircut, his crisply ironed shirts (thanks to Molly), and that legal brief-case he usually carried instead of a backpack.

"You're not?" Amber asked.

Nole shook his head. "Yeah, I guess we've gotten sort of close. He's kind of a strange dude, but he's smart and he's funny. He's a nice guy."

"Like you," Amber said.

Nole frowned at her. He stood up so abruptly his knee hit the table, and all the dishes rattled on the trays. His tea sloshed.

"I've gotta go."

Amber looked up at him. "It's like déjà vu."

"Huh?"

She waved him away. "Call me when you find your brain."

"Okay."

Nole strode away from the table and dumped his tray in the return area. The uneaten food earned him a stern glance from one of the round women with the hairnets who worked in the cafeteria. He didn't care.

He just had to—

What was that?

Nole stopped just outside the doors of the cafeteria and stared down the hall. He looked the other way, too. And then he turned to look behind him. He rubbed his eyes and checked the area again. Nothing was out of the ordinary. Dirty beige floor, pale yellow walls, posters vying for space on an overcrowded bulletin board that ran along the wall, a few students strolling in and out of the cafeteria— *nothing to see here, folks.* Yeah? So why was Nole sure he'd just spotted something big and black flutter around the corner at the end of the hall?

And what was that noise? Nole tilted his head and listened. It sounded like a rhythmic rustling, a sort of whispery sound like . . . well, like wet feathers being dragged along the floor.

Nole trotted out of the cafeteria building, stopped, bent over, and took a couple big breaths of fresh air outside.

"You okay, No?"

Nole looked up. One of his frat brothers, Steve, stood at the bottom of the stairs, his arm draped around a pretty, redheaded girl.

"Yeah, I'm fine."

"You say so," Steve said.

Nole lifted a hand, and Steve and the girl wandered off. Nole headed for the frat house.

Nole sat on his bed, his legs spread out and his hands loosely in his lap. He rolled his head around, listening to his neck crack, and he took several deep breaths.

When you're tense, adopt a relaxed posture, loosen your muscles, and breathe deeply, his mother taught him when he was little and was really worked up about something. *Tell your body how you feel, and it will come along for the ride.*

Usually that worked pretty well. But not this time. For good reason.

This situation was a little beyond old-school relaxation techniques. Between leaving the cafeteria and getting into this room, Nole had seen something—not someone, but *something*—following him four times. Four times!

Something. But what?

Four times, Sam heard that weird sound, a cross between the sound of the wind and a fluttering noise combined with regularly spaced airy thumps. No matter how many times he tried to tell himself he was hearing some kind of mechanical contraption or some sort of air-conditioning or fan unit attached to one of the buildings on campus, he couldn't convince himself of the lie. The truth was that he was hearing the sound of feathers, lots of them, brushing over the ground and grazing the edges of trees and buildings.

It might have been easier to believe his lies about the sound if he hadn't also seen a mammoth lurching swell of feathers rippling just at the edge of his peripheral vision. Four times, he'd seen these sinister forms billowing in and out between the trees and the buildings.

Well, *seen* was a bit of an overstatement. He actually wasn't sure about what his eyes had told him. The word *seen* implied a direct vision of something. Nole hadn't had that. He'd had this *idea* of seeing something. But the more he kicked around the idea, the more he became convinced he had *seen* something. Something had toyed with his senses, something just beyond the reach of confident visual surety. That something had been massive, black, and feathery.

And there it was again.

A large shape darkened Nole's small west-facing window, blotting out the sinking sun for just an instant. Nole only caught it out of the corner of his eye again, but it *was* there.

Nole bent over and put his head in his hands. "Oh man, oh man, oh man, oh man."

He straightened up. "Get a grip," he ordered himself.

Taking a deep breath, he looked around his room. Nole might have looked just sloppy enough to be cool, but he liked order in his surroundings. He was a minimalist. His room was soothingly white. The maple furniture had clean lines, though it was lightly stained. The small fridge he used for bottled water and the occasional leftover pizza (if he left it in the main kitchen, it was sure to get stolen) was white, with sleek lines. The bed was made, if a bit messily, and covered with a plain tan comforter. The rug under the bed was sisal. The floor and all furniture surfaces were clutter-free. The only things on his walls were a few black-and-white still shots from old movies. Nole's frat brothers kept trying to get him to hang the frat's Greek letters in his room. Nole said he didn't need them to know what frat he was in.

That refusal was just one of many that had earned him the nickname "No."

The black shape passed his window again.

Nole ran to the window and pulled the white room-darkening shade. A shadow flitted behind the shade, and Nole turned his back on the window.

"This is just stupid." He crossed to the bed and sat again. *Was it?*

Nole liked to think he was a pretty reasonable guy, but

he knew what was going on here, and it wasn't reasonable at all. It was very *unreasonable.*

It was unreasonable, but he was sure it was true: Nole was seeing Sam, in the Blackbird costume. And Sam was stalking Nole.

Why was Sam stalking Nole?

It was obvious, wasn't it? Sam was stalking Nole because he was now the Blackbird, and the Blackbird tortured those who confessed their dirty secrets.

So first Sam was going to toy with Nole the same way a bully toyed with his victim, and then Sam was going to kill Nole for being such a horrible person. Nole was sure of it.

And the worst part was that Nole deserved it.

Sunday nights in the frat house were movie nights, and normally, Nole didn't miss that—not just because he helped organize the events, but because he enjoyed them. But tonight's movie was a horror flick—with blood—and Nole wasn't up for it. He begged off, earning himself a shower of popcorn and a chorus of boos and hisses.

After a half hour of trying to study and another half hour of staring at the ceiling, Nole wished he had joined in movie night, but he didn't want to go down now. He was too edgy.

Nole's phone rang, and he snatched it up, hoping it was news about Sam. *Sam's all right. He is*, he thought before he said, "Hello."

"He is?" It was Amber.

"Who is?"

"You said, 'He is,'" Amber said.

He did it again? He really needed to stop saying his thoughts out loud.

"Wasn't I supposed to call you?" Nole asked.

"You didn't."

"I know."

"Jerk."

Nole's heart tried to strangle him. He swallowed to push it back into place.

"Maybe I had a reason," he said.

"I'm listening."

My friend has turned into a big blackbird and he's going to come and kill me, Nole thought. Then he gritted his teeth, waiting for Amber to tell him he'd said it out loud.

"Are you going for the obscene-phone-call technique?" she asked.

"What?"

"You're breathing heavily in my ear. It's not turning me on."

"Are you sure? Maybe there's a delayed reaction."

Amber laughed. "I'll let you know."

Nole grinned. In spite of how shaken he was, talking to Amber put him a little more at ease.

"I called because you seemed kind of freaked at the caf," Amber said.

"Um, I was just . . ." Just what?

"Is it about Sam?"

Nole gripped the phone so hard his fingers hurt.

"Uh, yeah."

Amber's voice softened. "I'm sorry."

"Thanks."

For a few seconds, they were both silent.

"Maybe you'll find it in your sleep," Amber said.

"Find what?"

"Your brain."

Nole grinned again. "I'll give it a go and let you know what happens."

"Be sure you do."

When Nole hung up the phone, he tried to convince himself that his thoughts about Sam were just some kind of craziness caused by shock. Maybe Amber was right. Maybe he could go to sleep and find his brain, the sane version of his brain, the one that wasn't being stalked by a friend in a bird suit.

It was worth a try. Nole stood and stripped out of his clothes.

Like the body-proud Ian, Nole slept in his underwear, but he wore boxer briefs, white. No rubber ducks.

Sliding in under wrinkled sheets that desperately needed a trip to the laundry, Nole took one last look around his room to be sure all was as it should be. It was. He closed his eyes.

At first, sleep wouldn't come. Nole's muscles wouldn't let go. They were so taut they could have been strung on a guitar and plucked, and if they'd been plucked, Nole was sure they'd sound dissonant. There was no question he was out of tune.

Nole tried closing his eyes. Sleep began to take him, and as soon as it did, images of implausibly huge wings scraped against his lids. Then he felt gigantic feathers battering against his entire body. He was being pummeled by stiff, elbow-length feathers. He could feel them drub against his skin in an eerie contrast of soft versus hard. How could something as light as a feather beat him with such power and force?

Fear pushed sleep from his consciousness. His eyes shot open.

Flailing for the switch on his nightstand lamp, Nole listened to the thundering pace of his heart.

Okay, that was alarming. Was that a dream?

No. It couldn't have been a dream because Nole had never fallen asleep. He'd just started falling asleep.

Nole stood up and got a bottle of water from his fridge. Downing half of it, he sat on the edge of the bed and steadied his breathing. It took several minutes, and he tried not to notice his hand was shaking when he took another sip of water.

Nole set down the water bottle, then said, "Get a grip."

He lay down once more.

"Let's try this again," Nole said to the room.

He reached over and turned off the light. He closed his eyes.

And someone, or something, opened the door to his room.

Nole catapulted from the bed and knocked over his lamp, trying to turn it on. The bulb hit the wood floor and broke, so Nole ran across the room and flipped the wall switch.

He was alone. The door to his room was closed. And it was locked.

Nole stared at his door.

What had just happened?

Nole looked around. In spite of how ordinary it looked, his room was suddenly threatening.

He needed a weapon.

Keeping one eye on the door, Nole crossed to his closet and picked up his aluminum softball bat. Holding it like a club, he sidestepped to the door. He got a tighter grip on the bat, then unlocked the door and threw it open.

The hallway was empty.

Ominous music wafted up from the first floor. Lots of bass and percussion. Nole looked at his watch. The movie was probably still going.

Nole backed into his room and closed the door. Locking it, he leaned against it and ran a hand through his hair. What was going on with him?

He looked at his bed. Then he stared at the doorknob. No way was he going to sleep unless he secured his door better.

Feeling a little like the idiot Sam used to say he was, Nole stepped over to his desk, grabbed his chair, and wedged the top of the back under the doorknob. Good thing he'd opted for a wooden chair instead of the plush one on wheels his mother thought he should get.

Once the chair was in place, Nole looked at the shade over the window. The window was locked, right?

Still clutching his softball bat, Nole checked the window. Yes, it was locked.

Good.

"Now can you stop acting like a paranoid mental patient?" he asked himself.

He didn't answer himself because he had no idea if he *could* stop. It didn't seem to be in his control.

Nole stood in the middle of his room for several more minutes. Then he decided there was no way he was going to sleep. So he righted his lamp and went into his closet for a broom, a dustpan, and a new bulb. After he cleaned up the broken bulb and put a new one in the lamp, he grabbed his laptop and got in bed with it. He might as well work on the new screenplay he was writing. He'd hoped it would be the script he and Sam would use for their midterm project. Now? Nole shrugged. Who knew what would become of it? But working on it might take his mind off his insanity. Or make him sleepy. Whichever came first would be fine with him.

It only took an hour for Nole to start nodding off. Encouraged by the silence, not just in his room but in the frat house as a whole, Nole set aside his laptop, made sure his baseball bat was leaning handily against the side of his bed, and switched off his lamp.

He immediately switched it back on.

Was that a shadow he saw right as the light was going out?

He scanned the room. Nothing. Of course.

Nole decided he needed a flashlight. His lamp might not survive the night if he kept lunging for it.

Opening his nightstand drawer, Nole got out the flashlight he kept there for power outages. It was amazing how often one of his frat brothers overloaded the circuits and blew the breaker. Setting the flashlight on the nightstand, Nole looked around one more time and then gingerly laid his head on the pillow. He remained there a few minutes, about as relaxed as the wooden Indian he'd accused Sam of being.

And *that* thought made him stiffen even more. His lungs seemed to have shrunk; they couldn't take in enough air.

He tried to blank out his mind.

Think of good things, his mom always said when he was little and he'd get upset. Then she'd sing that song she always sang when he needed cheering up. He never had the heart to tell her the song didn't do it for him. He wasn't that fond of rainbows or kittens.

But he did like Amber. He'd think about Amber.

Amber had freckles, just a few of them; they crossed the bridge of her nose like bird tracks.

Nole stiffened again.

"Ixnay on the irdsbay," Nole told himself.

He tried again. So Amber had these freckles, and she

had a matching trail of them across the top of her chest. He noticed them peeking out over the neckline of the white tank shirts Amber liked to wear. He also liked that about her—she stuck with jeans and white shirts. He'd never met a girl as unconcerned with fashion as she was. But she still managed to look great. Maybe it was the wild, shoulder-length, wavy blonde hair.

Nole's eyelids started to droop. Trying not to hold his breath, he reached out and turned off his lamp.

He lay still and listened. Nothing.

Good.

Nole closed his eyes . . .

. . . and the window swept open. Something hit the floor with a thud.

Nole grabbed for his flashlight, and he ended up knocking it across the room. He heard it clatter against the far wall. Nole seized his bat in the dark with his right hand and felt, with his trembling left hand, for the light. He managed to turn it on without breaking the bulb.

Light flooded the room and revealed . . . nothing.

"What the hell?!" Nole yelled.

He was *sure* he'd heard the window open. He *knew* he'd heard something hit the floor.

Did he dream it?

He shook his head.

No way. It had sounded too real.

Crossing to the window, Nole checked the lock again. It was latched.

Okay. Fine. He'd sleep with a light on. Didn't he tell Ian he could sleep through pretty much anything? And he could. So he would.

Nole retrieved his flashlight and set it on the nightstand. He repositioned his bat, and he lay down on the bed again.

He looked at his watch. It was only 11:25. Could he call Amber?

And say what? *Wanna come over and listen for invisible intruders with me?* There was a line he'd never tried before.

Nole threw his forearm over his eyes but kept his eyes open.

Why *did* he push Sam so hard yesterday?

Nole rolled over and punched the pillow. *Is this really the time for psychoanalysis?* he asked himself. He knew he shouldn't have taken that psychology class this semester. He did it because his adviser said psychology was helpful for all writers and filmmakers. He hadn't been prepared for how much it forced him to examine his own actions and motives.

But since he didn't want to close his eyes yet, why not ask the hard questions?

He'd known Sam was getting pissed off yesterday, but he'd kept needling him. Why?

And even more important, why had he enjoyed bullying Christine so much in junior high? What was it about her that brought out that level of cruelty?

Because there was no doubt about it. He'd been cruel, both in junior high and the day before.

What did he get from that? Did it make him feel better about himself?

He tried to remember something useful from his Psych 201 lectures. Was it mirroring? No. That was when you acted like someone else. Was it projecting? No. Wasn't that putting your feelings off on someone else? Displacement? Mm. Getting closer. That was taking out your frustrations and impulses on someone or something less threatening than what's bothering you.

Ah. He might be onto something.

But he was so tired.

Nole's eyes closed, and finally, he fell asleep.

A screeching squeal somewhere between an alarm's buzz and a siren's wail, a sound that barely came in under ear-damaging levels, wrenched Nole from cushy oblivion and hurled him back toward Earth. At the same time, a spine-scouring lightning strike burned an image of the Blackbird into Nole's brain, marking Nole's mind like a dreadful brand.

Nole fought to find his way back to full consciousness. But he couldn't get all the way there.

He was awake enough to know he'd been dragged from sleep, but that was as far as he could go. It was like something was holding him in place, clamping him into restraints in a way station between thought and no thought. He felt literally pinned to the bed. He could even feel the stabbing pressure of something sharp digging into his skin at the wrists and ankles.

He tried to buck off his assailant, but he couldn't move at all. He was utterly paralyzed. He could feel the pressure getting stronger and stronger, pushing him deeper into his mattress. He felt like he was being compressed into nothingness.

And still he tried to battle the force above him. He poured every ounce of his will into his muscles, and he grunted and strained to get free.

His confinement got worse, not better. Nole suddenly sensed an evil presence hovering over him. No, not hovering. Sitting. The presence was *sitting* on Nole's bed. Sitting on Nole! It was pressing down on him, engulfing him, insinuating itself into every part of him.

And then, with a flash of light, he was free. He busted loose from his bizarre captivity and awoke so fully that when he opened his eyes, he was completely alert, and he had his bat in his hands.

This was a good thing, because Nole was not alone in his room. A demonic presence of tenebrous feathers was poised right above his bed.

So Nole swung his bat.

In the nanosecond he swung, or was it the nanosecond *before* he swung, the thing above Nole's bed disappeared in an eruption of feathers that spewed throughout the room. Then the feathers vanished into nothingness.

It happened so fast, Nole couldn't be sure it happened at all.

All he could be sure of was that he did swing the bat. He

knew this because his lamp hit the floor. And another bulb bit the dust.

The time span in which Nole had seen the feathered thing was infinitesimal. It wasn't even a second. Nole's room went from sound and havoc to utter silence and stillness in the blink of an eye.

And yet . . .

And yet, the image of what Nole had seen in that blink was burned onto his retinas. Because he hadn't just seen feathers. He'd also seen soul-drilling, malevolent yellow eyes and a pointed, threatening beak. Those eyes had locked on to Nole's eyes. The sharp beak had aimed itself straight at Nole's guilty heart. Nole was sure it was the Blackbird, leaning over him with malicious intent. This wasn't just a still shot. This was a complete horror film playing out behind his eyeballs, in the theater of his own mind.

Without blood.

Sam was right. You didn't need blood to have horror. The creep factor was horrific enough.

Nole emitted a sound that was half moan and half laugh. It sounded like the strangled sob of an unhinged man.

How strange that in just a few hours, Nole had gone from a well-adjusted college guy to a paranoid mental case. Because he had to be crazy, right? To believe the horror that he and Sam had crafted on the fly had come to life?

Nole stood and paced around the room. Adrenaline was still coursing through his system, and he needed to get it out.

After three U-shaped passes back and forth around his bed, Nole decided one thing: His room was not big enough for his nervous energy. So Nole strode into his closet and grabbed sweats, a T-shirt, a hoodie, socks, and running shoes.

By the time Nole stepped into the bright hall, it was eerily silent in the frat house. He checked his watch again. It was almost 1:00 a.m.

Wait a second. Where did the last hour and a half go? Had Nole lain in bed thinking about psychology for that long . . . or had he been in that incapacitated state longer than he thought? He had no idea. The hammering of his heart was drowning out any rational thought at the moment.

Striding down the hall as quietly as possible, Nole darted to the stairs and ran down them without a sound. It wasn't that he cared about waking up his frat brothers; he didn't want to have to explain to anyone what he was doing. He just wanted to get away.

As soon as he stepped through the heavy double doors and onto the broad front porch of the frat house, Nole rethought his actions. Did he really want to go running in the dark with this creature hounding him? What if the thing got tired of toying with him and decided to grab him? What if it seized him and took off, the way an eagle snatched a rodent?

Now, that *did* sound insane. Did he really think the Blackbird was going to fly over and steal him off the ground? Even if some frightful rendition of Sam and his costume was coming after Nole, that didn't mean it could fly, did it?

Why not?

If any of what happened today was possible, then *anything* could be possible.

Nole turned and ran back up to his room.

He spent the next two hours trying to stay awake. He was too terrified to try and sleep again.

So he did push-ups and sit-ups. He listened to music. He played games on his computer. Finally, he started watching a movie.

The movie was what did him in. He had to close his laptop, and sleep overpowered him.

As soon as Nole closed his eyes, the high-pitched caterwauling sound started again. He tried to cover his ears, but again, he was paralyzed. Every time he tried to writhe against whatever force held him down, he had to push through the horror that still played in his head: the brutal eyes gazing into the murk of his very essence; the beak, like a scythe of judgment, cutting through his heart.

In his benumbed consciousness, inky feathered shapes streaked toward him, then retreated, over and over. He felt like a fat, helpless worm inching through the dirt—the Blackbird was merely playing with him before plucking him from the ground and swallowing him whole.

The sound and the image were tearing him apart from the inside. And still he fought, still he was held in place.

Until he wasn't.

As before, Nole came back into the land of the living with a crack of radiant light and a gaping silence. As before, he was on his feet immediately. And as before, the evil trespasser disintegrated into oblivion, as if it was never there. Which it clearly wasn't . . . even though every iota of Nole's being was arguing that it was.

Nole was going to lose his mind if he didn't get out of this room.

Once again, Nole opened his door and headed through the frat house. This time, when he got to the porch, he didn't let himself think. He just took off running down the brick path leading toward the quad. He had to get away, and that meant running.

The campus was dead still. Nole couldn't even hear a car in the distance. He wouldn't have been surprised to find out that the campus had been isolated under a glass dome.

But no, it was still in the real world. It seemed to be a perfectly normal campus, hanging out on Earth.

The night sky was black—clouds must have blown in. Bushes gyrated in a breeze that hadn't been blowing a few hours before. An occasional torn poster or candy bar wrapper skittered over the bricks.

The campus was lit by a series of wrought iron lampposts, which cast a mesh of shadow and light over the concrete and foliage. Nole found it mildly disorienting to look at—he seemed to see a feather in every blade of grass or errant branch.

So Nole kept his gaze directed at a spot on the ground fifteen or so feet in front of him, to try and keep his focus and also center his thoughts. He'd been running as fast as he could, as if running for his life.

He might have been running for his life. Something was torturing him, relentlessly. How could he escape it?

For now, he'd run.

Nole turned to look behind him, and his shoe caught a tree root. He tumbled off the path into the bushes. Lying on his back, holding a twisted ankle and wincing at the sharp pain that suggested he'd skinned his knees and his elbows, Nole threw his head back and shouted, "ENOUGH!"

He closed his eyes, and the horrendous sounds started again, the chilling, feathered entity loomed over him.

Nole opened his eyes, and of course, he was alone.

Nole fought his way out of the bushes, thrashing to his feet. Ignoring the throbbing pain in too many places to catalog, Nole said, "Sam, I'm sorry."

Turning in a circle, Nole said it again and again. Almost like a ritual. "Sam, I'm sorry." Quarter turn. "Sam, I'm sorry." Quarter turn. "Sam, I'm sorry."

Closing his eyes for a fraction of a second, Nole confirmed what he suspected, that his apologies weren't accomplishing anything at all. But he tried one more time. He threw his arms up to the sky and bellowed, "Sam, I'm sorry!"

This got a response. It got him a blinding flashlight

beam in the face and a campus cop's "Are you drunk or high?"

Nole rolled his eyes and faced the guy. He had dark skin and closely cropped hair. An unimpressive badge was clipped to his belt. "Neither," he said. "I was having nightmares, so I went for a run."

The campus cop shined his light from Nole's feet to the top of his head. Nole held his arms out away from his body, hands open to show he carried nothing.

"What's your name?" The cop put the light back in Nole's eyes.

Nole squinted and looked away, frowning at the spots that cavorted across his retinas. But hey, maybe if he was blind he wouldn't be able to see the Blackbird.

Even thinking the name made the image reassert itself.

"Name?" the cop repeated.

"Nole Markham. Could you please not shine that right in my eyes?"

The cop lowered the flashlight beam.

Nole couldn't see the cop's face very well, but he didn't look much older than Nole himself. He was much taller than Nole, though, and the way he loomed over the scene reminded Nole of—

Stop it! he commanded himself.

"Why were you yelling?" the cop asked.

"I was trying to get something out of my system."

The cop whipped the light back into Nole's eyes. "Drugs?"

"No. I'm not high. I'm not drunk. I . . . ." He hesitated.

"I did something to piss off a friend, and he's mad at me. I was just . . . I don't know."

The campus cop lowered the flashlight again. For a few minutes, they stood in silence. Nole noticed crickets chirping, which he hadn't heard while he was running.

Then the campus cop surprised him. He said, "I get that. You want to say you're sorry, but you're a little pissed that he's so pissed, so you're yelling that you're sorry to get that anger out of your system."

Nole lifted an eyebrow. Not bad for a campus cop.

"That's exactly right," he said.

"Okay, well, do you think you're done yelling?"

Nole nodded. "I can be, yes."

"Okay."

Nole waited to be sure the guy was done with him.

The cop gestured down the path with his flashlight. "I suggest you keep running. It's a great way to get stuff out of your system."

"Yeah. Thanks."

They nodded at each other, and Nole headed off again.

By the time he'd run a mile, the barest hint of pale pink was touching the top of the hills at the east edge of town. Dawn was coming. And Nole hadn't really slept at all.

Was he ever going to sleep again?

He had to let Sam know he was sorry . . . some other way than by screaming in the middle of campus. But how?

Nole was running back toward his frat house, when he heard footfalls approaching from the left. Slowing, trying not to quake in fear, Nole glanced in the direction of the footfalls. He tried to tell himself it sounded like a person, not a bird.

And he was right.

"Nole!"

For the first time in hours, Nole relaxed. He didn't relax completely, but he let go of enough anxiety to unkink the muscles in his neck and shoulders.

"Hi, Amber."

Amber jogged in place in front of him. Wearing dark blue sweats and a white T-shirt, she was just starting to work up a sheen of sweat.

"I've never seen you running in the morning before," Amber said.

"I don't run in the morning."

"Ah, so this must be another of your clones?"

Nole smiled, and when he realized how good it felt to smile, he smiled wider.

"Yes."

"How many do you have?"

"As many as I need for all the things I don't do."

Amber laughed. "Do you want to run with me, Nole's clone?"

"Sure."

Why not? Nole wasn't ready, not even a little, to face his day. He still hadn't come to terms with the night.

When they finished running, they ended up at the cafeteria again. "We have to stop meeting like this." Amber used the hem of her shirt to wipe sweat from her face.

"I've never met you here before," he said. "That was Nole's other clone."

"Right. I forgot."

The cafeteria doors were just opening. An enticing bacon aroma wafted out through the double doors. Only a few bleary-eyed students were starting to straggle toward the building. Amber put her foot up on the railing alongside the stairs and bent over to stretch.

Nole felt sweat trickling down his spine. He closed his eyes for a second and then immediately opened them wide to try and wake himself up. Then he wiped his eyes. They were dry and scratchy.

"Are you okay?" Amber asked. "I mean, seriously. You don't look too good."

"Well, thanks."

Amber gave him a half smile. "You know what I mean. Your eyes are really red."

"I haven't slept."

"All night?"

Nole shook his head.

"Anything I can do?"

Nole studied her. It was funny. Just now, he realized she reminded him a little of Christine, the girl he'd bullied in junior high. She had similar coloring, and her mouth was the same shape. He wondered if that's why he'd never thought of her as pretty until recently. Amber had been in several of his classes both the previous year and this one, and he'd never given her a second glance until a couple days before. Now, he realized, he liked her a lot.

With like came trust, so he blurted, "How would you fix it if you did something really wrong and it was a long time ago but then you did it again recently and you can't apologize to the person you just did it to, but you're sorry and you want to make amends somehow?"

Amber tilted her head and pursed her lips. "Guilt is keeping you awake?"

"Something like that."

Amber sat on one of the concrete steps and patted the space next to her. Nole acknowledged a greeting from a friend and sat next to Amber. The concrete was cold and damp.

"It's nice that you feel guilt. It shows character. A lot of guys are too stupid to know when they should feel guilty. I might have thought you were one of those."

"So why'd you want to go out with me?"

"I might have thought I was wrong."

Nole wasn't so sure she was. Did he feel guilty because he had character? Or because he didn't want to be murdered by the Blackbird?

"I think guilt is like a weed." Amber lifted her face to the sun, which was starting to climb above the tops of the trees. "It's best to pluck it out at the root."

"So apologize to the first person . . . the first person I need to apologize to," Nole said. "But how does that make amends with the second person?"

Amber said, "It's an energy thing. Yin and yang. Balance the scales in one place, and the balance radiates outward."

Nole wasn't so sure about that. But he had to do something.

"There you are."

Nole turned at the sound of a girl's voice.

It was Darla and their friend group. She pointed at Amber and said, "You weren't where we always meet."

Amber jumped up. "Sorry. It's his fault." She pointed at Nole and grinned.

He stood, too. "I need a shower."

Amber nodded and headed toward her friends. She turned back. "Good luck."

"Thanks." He knew he was going to need it.

How in the world was he going to find Christine Wilber?

Nole contemplated this question during his much-needed shower, and when he got back in his room, and when he stood at his window, watching people head to class. He'd already decided he was skipping all his classes for the day. Now he grabbed his laptop and prepared to find Christine. Looking at his bed longingly, Nole took his laptop to his desk. He was afraid if he even sat in bed, he'd start to fall asleep.

A quick internet search hadn't helped. Christine Wilber wasn't coming up on any searches. She apparently didn't do social media, and she hadn't done anything significant enough to get on a search engine's radar. So how could he find her?

A couple of Nole's frat brothers had been talking about Sam when Nole had returned to the frat house. Sam was still missing. So finding Christine was the only way for him to be safe again.

Or was he just coming unhinged?

What if the previous night had only been some simple sleep disorder caused by the shock of the day's news? He no longer felt like he was in shock, so maybe if he tried to sleep now, he'd be okay.

He hadn't seen any dark shadows or glimpses of big birds on his way back to the frat house. That was a good sign, wasn't it?

Nole closed his eyes just briefly and felt like he could fall asleep sitting up. Okay. That was it. He was going to lie down and go to sleep and forget all about Christine Wilber and Sam and the Blackbird. Since the only injuries he'd sustained in the harrowing hours of the long night were ones he caused himself, he had to conclude that the threat was in his head. And if it was in his head, he could darn well beat it.

Resolved, he set aside his laptop and got into bed, fully dressed in jeans and a white T-shirt. He sighed, stretching out. He put his head on the pillow, closed his eyes, and sleep took him . . .

Right into hell.

The second Nole's brain waves slowed, the Blackbird

appeared in a dissonant din of keening and buzzing that was so intense it felt like a physical invasion boring into Nole's ear canal. Diabolical wings leaned over Nole menacingly.

Aiming its beak directly at Nole's right eye, the Blackbird bent even closer. Nole knew his eye was closed because he was asleep, but in the dream world, his eyes were open to see the beak move lower and lower. At the same time, the weight ramming down on him got heavier and heavier. Nole's chest was being crushed under the feathered mass.

Even though he knew it would do no good, Nole wriggled and jerked himself back and forth, trying to throw off the hideous creature. He concentrated on trying to free his legs, but that just made things worse. His legs started to spasm, and it felt like someone was trying to tear them off his body. The pain in his limbs was excruciating.

The sound morphed, too. The high-pitched tones abated, only to be replaced by a combination of crackling static and a loud hum, interrupted at regular intervals by a deafening *ZAP* sound that reminded Nole of the electric bug zappers his grandfather kept by his back deck. Only this *ZAP* was not designed for mosquitoes. It was tuned to something the size of a pterodactyl.

Nole realized that he could no longer breathe. The weight on his chest was flattening his lungs and stopping his heart. He felt like he was being dragged into some other realm, the Blackbird's realm. And as he left his world, the world he realized he'd taken for granted all his life, his body began to tingle. The tingles sped up, and they became vibrations so fast and powerful it felt like every cell in his body was palpitating at a jackhammer pace. Faster and faster, his body vibrated, and it began to emit a droning sound.

Burrrrrrrrrrrrrr.

Nole tried to scream, but he couldn't even use his mouth. He realized he couldn't even *feel* his mouth . . . or the rest of his body. He wasn't just paralyzed. He was numb!

All that was left of Nole was his consciousness. His mind was still functioning fine; in fact, it was functioning too well. It was giving him a relentless rundown on the system-wide failure of his body.

Nole's existence receded further and further into an inky, feathered oblivion. The noise crescendoed. The pain intensified. Nole was sure he was on the verge of total annihilation.

And then it all stopped . . .

Except for a vise grip on his arm, an annoying jostling of his shoulder, and the sound of someone yelling, "DUDE!!!!"

Nole opened his eyes.

Ian let go of his arm and shoulder, and backed away from the bed.

"Dude," he repeated, but at a lower volume.

Nole realized he was bathed in sweat. His skin felt clammy, and his clothes stuck to him. He ached all over.

"Are you okay?" Ian asked.

Nole couldn't answer that question, so he just shook his head and then nodded. That should clear things up.

Ian, wearing only red boxer shorts covered with charging bulls, dropped into Nole's desk chair. Nole looked at him. He'd never seen the big guy look so shook up. He'd never seen Ian in his room before, either. They only hung out when other frat brothers were around, usually in the main lounge downstairs.

"How'd you get in here?" Nole asked.

Ian blinked, then twisted his mouth in a guilty-little-kid way. "Oh, I sort of broke your door."

Nole looked over to see his doorjamb splintered and his door hanging on one hinge.

"Sorry," Ian said. "I thought you were dying."

Nole returned his gaze to Ian and raised an eyebrow.

"I've never heard anyone make a sound like that, dude," Ian said. "It was *loud* but really low, like grunting sort of, like you were trying like crazy to scream but someone had their hand over your mouth. And there were all these thuds and thumps. I thought someone was trying to kill you. So I broke the door to get in."

Tears filled Nole's eyes. He was weirdly touched.

Then fizzes of terror skirted along his skin. What if he had been dying? What would have happened if Ian hadn't busted into his room to wake him? Would the Blackbird have been able to take Nole to another . . . what? Dimension? Realm? Level of hell?

He realized Ian was waiting for him to say something. "Thanks, Ian. I was stuck in a really nasty nightmare. You got me out of it."

Ian shrugged. "Well, good. It seemed pretty bad." He looked hard at Nole. "Are you sure you're okay?"

Nole nodded. "Nothing a hot shower and some food won't solve." He sat up. He tried to ignore the room-spinning sensation that triggered a wave of nausea.

Ian stood. "Okay. Well . . ."

Nole wasn't sure he could stand yet, so he didn't.

"Sorry about your door," Ian said. "I can fix it for you." He strode to the door and looked at it. "I just need to get a couple things from the hardware store."

"You don't need to do that. It's my fault you broke it."

Ian shook his head. "Nah. I want to. I like fixing things. It'll take my mind off the makeup test I have later today. I need to pass it so I can keep playing ball."

Nole nodded. "Let me know if you ever need any help with, um, classwork."

Ian looked closely at him, probably to see if Nole was jerking his chain. He wasn't. He might have been the day before, giving the dumb jock a hard time. But not today.

Ian nodded. "Thanks." He went through the now unguarded opening to Nole's domain.

"Uh, Ian?" Nole called.

"Yeah?" Ian turned.

"If you had to find someone from your past, like from

junior high or something, what would you do? I mean, if they weren't online?"

"Um, I don't know. Do you know their parents?"

Nole snapped his fingers. "That's brilliant. Yes, thanks. Great. Thanks again, Ian, for breaking in."

Ian shrugged. "Anytime."

"I hope not," Nole muttered when Ian went back to his own room.

Nole stood, and for the second time that day, he headed for the showers. In the shower, he chastised himself for being so dense. He knew Christine Wilber's parents were still in town because her dad owned Wilbers' Eats, a popular greasy-spoon diner downtown. How could Nole have forgotten that? One of the things he'd often said to Christine when he was bullying her was "So you've eaten everything on your dad's menu, a thousand times; what do you recommend?"

Nole groaned at the memory and turned the water to cold. He flinched when the icy bite shocked his skin. But he both needed and deserved the jolt. It would help him do what he now knew he needed to do.

Nole was relieved to find Wilbers' Eats mostly empty when he arrived. Only one silver vinyl booth was taken, by an elderly couple picking through scrambled eggs and hash browns. And only one red vinyl stool was occupied, by a sleepy-looking guy in a janitor's uniform. He was drinking coffee and methodically plowing through a large piece of cherry pie.

The diner smelled like a diner, a good one. The aromas came from the food—a weird but not unpleasant mix of onions, fried chicken, apples, and chocolate—and the coffee, not from grease. Clunking and sizzling sounds came from behind a low divider wall separating the dining room from the kitchen. There was a large pass-through for the food, and next to it hung one of those carousel things to clip orders to. It was empty.

A thin woman with limp dyed-blonde hair, turned to greet Nole when he entered. "Sit wherever you want." She waved a hand and returned to her chore, starting a new pot of coffee. The woman wore a pinkish uniform dress and a bright blue apron. Her name tag read LOIS.

Nole didn't want to sit. He wanted to get on with it. So he approached the counter near an old-fashioned cash register. He shifted from one foot to the other.

Lois turned and raised an eyebrow. "Did you want takeout?"

"No. Thank you. I, um, need to see Mr. Wilber. Is he here now?"

Lois chuckled. "Sure he is. He practically lives here now. He does all the cooking." Lois rotated toward the kitchen and shouted, "Earl, get out here. Someone's asking for you."

Nole clenched his fists. He wasn't looking forward to this conversation.

He looked up and watched a very short man push through a swinging door to the right of the food pass-through. No wonder Nole hadn't gotten a glimpse of the man. He was barely five feet tall. And he was thin. *That* was a surprise.

"Hello, sir." Nole held out his hand. "My name's Nole Markham."

Earl Wilber grinned and shook Nole's hand. "Good to meetcha."

Earl was missing a front tooth, but somehow that added to his friendly smile. Unlike his fair-haired daughter, Earl had brown hair and brown eyes. But Nole could see Christine in the man's face. Or would that be the other way around? Both had bow-shaped mouths, wide cheek-bones, and close-set eyes.

"What can I do for you?" Earl Wilber asked. His manner was deferential.

Nole had been trying to think of a smooth way of bringing up the subject of finding Christine, and he hadn't come up with a thing. So he just burst out with it: "Sir, I need to find your daughter, Christine, and I was hoping you could tell me where she is."

Earl Wilber's friendly expression didn't change. He just said, "That right?" He leaned an elbow on the counter across from Nole. Nole noticed Earl Wilber's forearm was cross-hatched with little burn scars. From short-order cooking?

"And why is that?" Earl asked.

"You sweet on her?" Lois asked. Her voice was low and scratchy.

Earl laughed and patted her shoulder. "Well, now, Lois, I expect that's his business."

Outside, the sun disappeared so abruptly everyone in the diner turned to look through the picture window. Black storm clouds were tumbling across the sky. Beneath the clouds, right outside the diner, a huge hunched and feathered form shuffled past.

What?

Nole did a double take. Had he just seen that, or had he imagined it?

He looked around to check if anyone else had seen it. The elderly woman in the booth was looking past the elderly man's shoulder, her gaze focused on the clouds and her face pinched in what could have been fear or worry. But maybe she just didn't like storms.

Whether he saw it or made it up, Nole had a feeling he needed to get a move on.

Looking back at Christine's dad, Nole said, "I'm going to tell you the truth, even though it makes me look, like, really bad. But . . ." He shrugged. "I was in junior high with Christine, and I was, well, I was a bully. I wasn't nice to her at all, and I need to tell her how sorry I am that I was so, like, mean to her."

"Is this one of those make-amends things?" Lois asked Nole.

"Not in any official way. I just . . . need her to know I'm sorry."

Earl Wilber rubbed his jaw. "You the boy who threw burrs at her?"

Nole scrunched up his face in pure embarrassment. He looked down. "Yeah. That was me."

When Earl Wilber didn't say anything, Nole looked up at the man. He expected to see anger in the man's eyes, but all he saw was compassion.

Earl Wilber held his gaze for several seconds. Nole squirmed, but he didn't break off the connection. He had to face what he'd done. What better way than looking his victim's father in the eye?

Finally, Earl Wilber said, "Okay. I'll tell you where she is."

"She's such a sweet girl," Lois said.

Nole ignored his sudden nausea and accepted the directions Earl Wilber gave him. Then he went outside, making sure he didn't look up as he hurried to his car.

Nole's car wasn't much of a car. Truthfully, it was basically a piece of junk on wheels. It was such a piece of junk, in fact, that Nole never admitted he even owned the car. He kept it at his grandfather's house, and he only drove it when necessary. When the car was built—many, many years before—it had been a cool car. But too many owners, too many miles, too many fender benders, and just plain too much time had turned the car into a barely-hanging-together collection of rusted red metal and engine parts that only just managed, most of the time, to get Nole where he needed to go.

Today, he was going to be pushing it. He only had to go about thirty-five miles, but the small campus where

Christine was a sophomore, like Nole, was up in the mountains. The school was a music-and-arts college, according to Christine's dad.

The storm clouds were still hanging around, and they made Nole very, very nervous. Whenever he accidentally glanced up at the sky, he saw feathered wings beating the billowing clouds. He also kept seeing an immense black-feathered shape shambling along in the wake of his straining vehicle. Every time that happened, he pushed the accelerator pedal harder, which didn't help at all because he already had it pressed to the floor. Nole's car was struggling, predictably, with the uphill drive.

After about fifty minutes, however, Nole arrived at a fancy modern cement archway over a narrow road that led into a small collection of glass-and-cement sculptural structures that nearly sang out, "Artsy." As Earl Wilber had instructed, Nole followed the road to the left as it wove through two inverted-triangle-shaped buildings and took Nole right into the parking lot of an asymmetrical four-story dorm.

As soon as Nole turned off his car, thunder rumbled in the not-nearly-far-enough-away distance. A big drop of water hit Nole's arm as he got out of the car. Refusing to look around, he trotted toward the dorm, but even without seeing his oppressor, he knew it was there. He could hear the laborious lugging of feathers across the pavement, and he could feel the air currents behind and around him shift as his hunter closed in.

Nole was sweating by the time he got inside the dorm. The nausea that had started in the diner had grown and been joined by a pounding headache. Now Nole was starting to feel light-headed. He had to hurry.

Practically running through a sprawling lounge, his shoulder blades tingling with the sensation of being tracked, Nole glanced at a few girls sprawled on plush sectional sofas, chattering away. Oddly, he realized as he put the lounge behind him that he had no idea what the girls looked like or what they were wearing. He felt like his eyesight was getting blurry.

The building smelled like cloves, and it was remarkably quiet for a dorm. Only the faintest hint of a staccato beat could be heard from a distance.

It was a little after 5:00 p.m., and Earl Wilber had told Nole that Christine was nearly always in her dorm that time of the day because she ate early, before going to practice. Earl didn't say what kind of practice.

Nole easily found the room number Earl had given him. Leaning against the wall to steady himself, Nole raised a hand and knocked.

"Come in," a cheerful, musical voice called.

It sounded a little like Christine, but it was too upbeat to be her.

Nole opened the door, looked around the room, and froze, staring.

The room had only one person in it, a girl. And the girl was obviously Christine. He might have doubted that if he hadn't just been with Earl Wilber, but this girl had her dad's features, if not his coloring.

Christine was still as blonde and freckled as she'd been in junior high school. She still had the slightly crooked teeth he remembered. But otherwise, she was a very different Christine Wilber.

"Hi. Are you looking for Claire?"

"Huh?"

"My roommate?"

Nole shook his head. He was having trouble staying upright. His legs felt weak, and something pushed against his back and down on his shoulders as if trying to pile-drive him into the floor.

"Then who you are you looking for?" Christine asked. She twisted her nose in the twitchy way she did when they were in junior high, but she didn't seem to see anything behind Nole.

He tried to tell himself, for the hundredth time, that he was imagining things.

When Nole didn't answer, Christine said, "I think you have the wrong room?" She tilted her head with her sentence/question.

Christine sat at a school desk similar to Nole's. She had a book open in front of her, and she held a plastic container of salad. It was nearly empty.

When Nole didn't answer Christine, she looked down and forked up a cucumber. She bit into the cucumber, and its distinctive scent filled the air. So did her crunching sounds.

Nole kept staring.

Christine Wilber sat cross-legged on her desk chair, and one of her bare feet kept time with music that must have been in her head. She wasn't wearing earbuds. She was dressed in a full-length, skintight light blue leotard.

Christine Wilber wasn't overweight anymore. She was obviously as fit as Nole was.

That wasn't the only way she was different. Although she still had the same facial features and quirky expressions, Christine held herself with an air of confidence that made it clear she was a very different girl from the one he'd known in junior high. Nole's mental processors were struggling to keep up with the unexpected information. His neuropathways were announcing, "This input does not compute."

"Do you talk?" Christine asked. She hesitated and worked her mouth as if trying to find the right words. Then she said, "I'm not being mean or anything. It's just that you're standing there staring." She clasped her hands together and shrugged.

Nole shook his head to try and reset his circuits. "You don't remember me?" he asked.

"*That's* the first thing you say?" Christine laughed.

He remembered that laugh. He'd only heard it once in junior high, when he'd watched her play with a ferret someone had brought to show-and-tell. Her laugh was a pleasing trill that made you want to laugh, too.

She set down her salad. "Okay, let's see." She stared at him, then shook her head. "No, I don't remember you. Should I?"

"I would."

"You would what?"

"I'd remember me. If I were you, I mean." Nole pressed his hand to his forehead.

Christine shrugged again. "Why don't you just tell me who you are?"

Nole blew out air. "Okay."

A couple girls came down the hall behind Nole. They were singing at the top of their lungs. He waited until they were well past, trying to ignore the fact that they'd been followed by that swishing, thumping sound that told him his feathered nemesis was nearby.

He opened his mouth, and he found he couldn't get the words out. His eyes filled with tears, and he had to swallow.

Christine frowned. "Hey, are you okay?"

Nole's eyes got even wetter. She was so nice.

"I was the guy who bullied you in junior high." He said the words fast, sort of like peeling off a guilt bandage.

"Which one?" Christine asked.

Nole blinked.

She shrugged and twitched her nose. "The Hate-on-Christine crew was pretty big."

"I started the 'Sh' thing, and I threw burrs on you." Nole felt like he was about an inch tall. He couldn't understand why he'd ever thought it was so funny . . . either when he did it or when he told Sam about it.

"Oh, that was you?" She focused her small blue eyes on him. "I'm sorry. I've forgotten your name."

"Nole Markham."

She nodded. "I think I remember you. You didn't have all that hair then. You were skinnier, too. No muscle."

Nole blushed. He had been pretty slight in junior high. What had made him think he was so great he could make fun of someone else? He wiped his still-wet eyes.

Christine stood and skipped across the room toward him so quickly it was like she flew. She was extraordinarily elegant and precise in her movement.

Nole stiffened, not sure what she was going to do.

She hugged him.

This wasn't at all how he had thought this would go.

At first, Nole just stood there, his arms rigid at his sides. But then the combination of her sincere kindness and the honey-sweet scent of her hair released him from his resistance. He hugged her back, blinking away his tears.

Christine let him go and stepped away. She was so close he could see all her freckles and a few dark flecks in her blue eyes.

"That wasn't an *I forgive you* hug," she said. "It was a thank-you."

"What?"

Christine motioned for him to come into the room, and he did, sitting on her roommate's desk chair when Christine pulled it out. She returned to her desk, sat, and rotated her chair to face Nole.

Clasping her hands together, she said, "I'm not going to

tell you this to let you off the hook for bullying, but it looks like you really are sorry."

"I really am," Nole said sincerely. He was surprised by how truly sorry he was.

She nodded, thought for a few seconds, then said, haltingly, "I'm going to tell you this just because I learned something from it, and I figure maybe I can pass it on. In junior high, my mom was always on my case about everything. I felt like crap about myself. You and the others kept putting me down, which also didn't help. To be honest, I barely remember you. But I remember how bad I felt all the time. Eventually, though, I stopped feeling bad, and I got angry. I decided to treat myself well. I like to dance, and I started dancing to have fun, you know, just alone in my bedroom. But then I started going to a real studio, and I found out that I'm actually pretty good at it. When the music swept me up, nothing else mattered. Of course, my mom loved that dancing helped me lose weight, but that wasn't enough to make her happy. I think part of me will always struggle on some level with that."

Nole stood, opened his mouth to protest.

She came over and waved him off. "Don't. It's okay. See? That's the thing. All that bullying forced me to step up and love myself—no matter what I see in the mirror or what people say about me. I know my value. I'm actually here on a dance scholarship. So see? Sometimes when something bad happens, it leads to something good."

Nole nodded.

Christine looked directly at him. "And I do forgive you. You can let it go. I'm fine."

Nole's eyes teared up again. He wiped them with the back of his hand.

Christine looked over Nole's shoulder. She patted and squeezed his hand. Then he walked out into the hallway, and she closed her door.

Nole sagged against the wall. That's when he realized he no longer felt a presence lingering nearby.

No more feathers.

The hallway was silent.

His headache was gone. Nole rolled his head from side to side and shrugged, then released his shoulders. His tension was gone, too. It was all gone. He felt like he'd just set down a backpack full of bricks.

Nole smiled a little and picked his way through the dorm. In the lounge, he waved at the girls. He could see them clearly now. They were dressed in leotards like Christine's.

Outside, Nole wasn't surprised to find the sun plowing its way through the clouds. He closed his eyes and breathed in air scented by the miniature carnations growing in a planter at the edge of the parking area. He hadn't noticed those on the way in.

He started toward his car, and his phone rang. Reaching in his pocket, Nole pulled out his phone and answered it. "Hello?"

The first two words spoken into his ear brought Nole to

a stop. As he listened, he started grinning. Then he said, "I'm on my way!"

He ran for his car.

Sam was waiting for Nole in front of the film studies building when Nole got back.

"Sam!" Nole shouted. He ran toward his friend.

Sam raised a crutch and waved it in the air, then put it back down when Nole reached him. Nole grabbed Sam and hugged him. As best he could, Sam hugged him back enthusiastically.

"There's my favorite idiot," Sam said. "Where were you? You didn't say."

"I went—" Nole waved the air. "It doesn't matter. What happened to you?"

Sam rolled his eyes. "Apparently, I've been hanging around you too long. Idiocy must be catching."

Nole smacked Sam's shoulder.

"Ow. Hey. Wounded guy here." Sam winked. "Seriously, I was being dumb. I was walking on the tracks with headphones on."

"Dumb is one word for it."

Sam laughed. "Yeah. Right? So I turned around just in time to see the train, and I jumped off the tracks, but jumping has never been something I'm good at, so not only did something on the train gouge my arm as I leaped"—he lifted a bandaged arm—"I lost my balance and fell down the embankment and broke my leg. If

I'd had normal-size legs, I probably would have been fine."

Nole laughed. "You and your legs. Get over it."

Sam ignored Nole. "I was trying to drag myself back up when I slipped and ended up sliding all the way down into the culvert. Then I passed out. I guess I was pretty well hidden. I never heard anyone calling for me, and no one saw me until early this morning, when my parents came back with a couple cops to search again." Sam punched Nole's arm. "I'm so happy to see you, man."

"Not as happy as I am to see you." Nole realized he meant that, really meant it. "And I'm sorry." He wasn't taking any chances. Just because Sam was here didn't mean the Blackbird was gone.

"For what?"

"For being such a jackass about the bullying thing. You're right. It's not funny."

Sam waved the air with his crutch again. "I was over-sensitive about it. It's no big deal."

"No," Nole said. "Being thoughtless *is* a big deal."

Sam shook his head. "I won't disagree with that, but I shouldn't have thrown stones at a glass house."

"Huh?"

"I never answered you when you asked if I had secrets."

Nole waited.

Sam leaned in. "Remember I said I was bullied?"

Nole nodded.

"Well, I got revenge on one of my bullies by bullying him right back. I played a really mean joke on him just before freshman year."

"Jerk."

Sam laughed. "Back atcha."

"Nah," Nole said. "No more jerk clones."

"What?"

Nole laughed. "Oh, it's a joke between Amber and me."

"'Amber and me,' huh? I want to hear about that. Want to grab a pizza?"

"Sure, I'm starving. I haven't eaten since before noon."

"Why not?"

"Long story. Maybe I'll tell you sometime."

"The Blackbird will make you tell," Sam said.

Nole's heart stuttered, but then Sam laughed.

The child's bedroom was crowded, even though it held only two people. It was crowded because it held so many hopes and so many regrets. It was crowded because it held the potential for so much more than what was.

"Let's get you comfy." Margie cradled Jake's shoulders while she reached behind him and repositioned his pillows. The window fan blew a lock of her shoulder-length light brown hair across her upper lip so it looked like she had a mustache. She pursed her full lips and puffed the hair back in its place.

Jake tried to remember the last time he'd been comfy. Maybe three years ago, when he was six?

No matter what Margie did with the pillows, Jake wouldn't be comfy, but he let Margie think she was doing something helpful. She tried really hard, and he didn't want her to know she couldn't make it better, like she wanted to.

Over the whirr of the fan, Jake could hear kids playing in the neighbor's yard. Squeals of glee alternated with laughter and the occasional shout. He tilted his head so the elm tree outside his window wasn't in the way, and he saw the trailing end of a sprinkler spraying a stream of water across the neighbor's lawn. Actually, he saw two, but he knew one was just an echo of the first. Although the fan drowned it out, the sprinkler made its *pft, pft, pft* sound in his mind. He loved that sound. It was the sound of fun. He used to be one of the kids who played in that sprinkler and squealed in glee. When it got over ninety degrees, Mrs. Henderson always let the kids turn her front yard into a water park.

"Jake?"

Jake shifted his attention from the window to Margie. Margie had an echo, too. Both Margies frowned at him. Jake concentrated on ignoring the second

Margie, as he had to ignore the second one of everything he saw.

His Pine Nut made him see double. It was annoying, but he was used to it.

Margie rubbed Jake's bald head. Her palm was warm and rough, so different than his mom's palms had been. He wasn't sure he had it right because it had been four years since his mom had died, but he remembered his mom's hands as soft. Still, he liked it when Margie rubbed his head. It got him a tiny bit closer to finding comfy's hiding place.

"Earth to Jake."

Obviously, she'd been talking and he hadn't heard her. He did that more and more these days. He was happier when he was not where he was, so it was hard to make himself pay attention to what she was saying.

"I asked if you feel up to some vegetable soup." Margie blew her hair off her face again as she fussed over Jake's sheets. Her full cheeks were flushed from the heat, and her mascara was smudged.

Jake thought it was funny that Margie always wore makeup. It wasn't like many people saw her. Mostly, it was just Jake.

"I think you're pretty without makeup," he once told her. "You have such big eyes. You look like a cartoon princess."

Margie had obviously liked that, but she still wore makeup. "It's a girl thing," she told him. He figured she wore makeup in case some handsome guy came to the door. When he said that, though, she'd laughed and said, "I'm not in the market for a handsome guy. I'm only twenty-seven. I'm still young. You're all the handsome guy I need."

Jake didn't think twenty-seven sounded young. That was three times older than he was now, and Margie was three years older now because she'd been taking care of him ever since comfy became part of his past.

Jake didn't want to be trouble, but it was too hot for soup and he wasn't sure he could keep it down. "Crackers?" he asked.

Margie sat down on the edge of the bed. She always sat there, even though a green-and-blue-plaid plush chair was right next to the other side of the bed. The smiley face on her T-shirt twisted so it looked like it was winking at Jake. Sometimes, Jake winked back, but he didn't feel like it today. He was doing that thing that Margie said he should never do.

"No me-woe," she always said. "Otherwise known as 'feeling sorry for yourself,' 'having a pity party,' 'woe is me,' and 'oh, the drama!'"

That used to make Jake laugh. Today, not so much.

Outside, one of the twins from across the street laughed; she had a weird laugh that sounded like a cuckoo clock, so Jake recognized it. He shifted his gaze to the window again.

Margie leaned toward Jake and gently used her fingers

to turn his face back toward her. "I know it's been a long time since you've been able to play with your friends, but you'll be out there with them in no time. You'll see."

Jake nodded, even though he didn't agree with her.

Margie was a big fan of positive thinking. She was always saying things like "Today is a day for miracles," and "Things are looking up," and "This too shall pass," and "All is well," and "It's always darkest before the dawn." She had like a gazillion smiley-face T-shirts with various hats or outfits or expressions. Jake once asked where she got them, and she said a friend who had a T-shirt company made them for her. She had one made for Jake, a smiley face wearing a baseball cap with his favorite team's logo. He used to wear it a lot, but he hadn't wanted to put it on for a while.

When Jake didn't say anything, Margie said, "Okay, crackers it is."

"Thanks," Jake said.

She patted his knee. Then she waved at a fly. "How did you get in here?" she asked it.

Jake looked at a dime-size hole in his screen, but he didn't give the fly's secret away. He liked it when flies visited. He liked watching them flit around the room, and he liked listening to them buzz. A couple years before, his dad got him a laptop and a tablet to use for doing his lessons and to look stuff up. He always kept the tablet in the bed with him, because he had so many questions about everything, and the tablet was like a magic portal to answers.

The tablet told him that flies only live twenty-eight days. Less than a month. He figured that was why they were always darting around. They had to hurry up and live as much as they could while they had the chance. It made him feel stupid for lying around so much. Why wasn't he hurrying like the flies?

Well, because he couldn't.

Jake noticed Margie was heading toward the door of his room, her arms full of towels she'd used to clean up his mess. This was day two of the latest round, and it was worse than most day twos.

"Margie?"

Margie turned. She flashed him her wide smile. "What, kiddo?"

"When is Dad calling?"

Margie's smile wavered. "I'm not sure, sweetie." She set the towels down on the desk he hadn't used for a while now, and she came back to the bed. She sat down again. "You know he calls whenever he can, right?"

Jake nodded.

"And you know he thinks about you all the time?"

Jake frowned and shook his head. "I don't think he does."

Margie raised an eyebrow. "Why not?"

"Well, he's a good soldier, right?"

"Of course he is."

"So he has to concentrate on what he's doing. I bet he doesn't think about me when he's concentrating on his job.

But that's okay. I don't want him to think about me and end up shooting himself in the foot or something." Jake strained so he could lift his arms and pretend to shoot his foot. He gave Margie a weak grin.

Margie laughed. "No, that would be bad."

Jake joined her when she went on. "Very, very bad."

They laughed together.

"I'll go get those crackers." Margie stood, leaned over, and kissed Jake's forehead.

He noticed her eyes got teary when she looked into his eyes. He understood why, so he didn't say anything. Instead, he asked, "Can you bring extra crackers?"

"Sure. Are you extra hungry?"

"Not really. I've just been thinking it's wrong for me not to offer something to Simon when he visits. You're supposed to do that, right? Offer food or drinks or stuff to guests?"

Margie raised an eyebrow. "I didn't know that Simon ate."

Jake laughed. "That's just silly. Of course he eats."

"I thought he lived in the cabinet."

"Yeah. So?"

Margie tilted her head. "So there's food in there?"

Jake shrugged. "I don't know where he gets his food. But yesterday, we talked about what kind of cake we like. He likes chocolate, just like I do."

"Simon likes chocolate, huh?"

"Yep. And peanut butter. Just like me. But he doesn't

like it with banana. He says if he gets a banana-nut sandwich, he takes off the bananas."

"Oh, he does, does he?"

Jake nodded.

Margie shook her head and smiled. "Okay. Extra crackers it is, then."

"Really?"

"Well, we can't be rude to Simon." Margie winked.

Jake shook his head. "No. I'll need to apologize to him,
too."

"Why?"

"Because I haven't offered him anything yet."

"I'm sure he's not upset about it."

Jake frowned. "I hope so."

Margie squeezed his foot. "I *know* so." She headed to the
door.

Jake watched her cross the few feet between his bed and
the desk, where she left the towels. Above the towels, a
poster of his favorite robot character bubbled in the humid
air. One corner of it fluttered in the fan's breeze.

When Margie left the room, Jake looked around at all
his posters. They had a dual theme going: science fiction
movies and baseball. A painting that combined his two
favorite things hung above the little white cabinet on
the wall opposite his window. His dad had an artist friend
do the painting: It showed a baseball game being played on
the moon. Jake wished he'd be around to see that in real
life. But he wouldn't.

Jake rolled his eyes at himself. "Oh, the drama!" he said out loud.

He surveyed his room again. His green baseball-patterned curtains gyrated in a spastic rhythm that matched his fan's rotations. Jake looked back toward his baseball-on-the-moon picture. Then he looked at his little cabinet.

The cabinet, which was about three and a half feet tall and maybe two feet wide, had been in Jake's room when his parents got this house—at least that's what his dad said. Jake didn't use the cabinet. It was just there, and normally, he didn't give it a thought . . . until recently. Now the cabinet was becoming important to him, because his new friend, Simon, lived in it.

Jake picked up his tablet. He wanted to see if he could beat yesterday's score on his math game. When the tablet came on, he looked at the time. Good. It was after five. Bedtime was only four hours away.

Jake loved bedtime. It was his favorite part of the day. Well, that and sleep itself. Sleep was way more fun than being awake. He could do things in his sleep he couldn't do when he was awake. But bedtime was even better than sleep. That was when Simon came to visit.

In the basement, Margie put the latest load of towels in the old washing machine and started it up, patting the scarred white lid affectionately when the machine began the cycle with its usual efficiency. Margie was pretty sure the machine, and its pal, the battered dryer next to it, were relics from another era, but they weren't giving up yet. That was good because taking care of Jake involved a lot of laundry, and Margie was pretty sure Evan, Jake's dad, couldn't afford to replace a washer and dryer. She was pretty sure Evan, at his rank, could barely afford *her*. He paid her better than most would pay, and the truth was that at this point, if she could have, she'd have worked for free. She loved Jake like a son.

And that's what was making it all so hard.

Margie sat down in the faded blue webbed lawn chair that was set up, for reasons she never understood, in front of the shelves by the stairs. She had to go up and get Jake his crackers, but she needed a minute.

The basement was cool compared to the rest of the house. Not for the first time, she wished they could set up Jake's bed down here. His room had western exposure and it got so hot in the afternoons. But it was too damp down here. The radiation and chemo had annihilated Jake's immune system. A simple cold could kill him.

Margie blinked away tears and stared at the tools, games, and camping gear stacked on metal shelves against the wall. A couple dozen boxes labeled by year hinted at the memories this family had made before everything got turned on its head. First, Jake's mom was killed. Then he got sick. It wasn't fair.

Margie pulled out her cell phone, clicked on her recording app, and started talking. "Day two of the latest round of chemo. Dr. Bederman is hopeful, but he told me today that Jake can only have two more rounds. They've already gone beyond the usual number of treatments for this protocol. The tumor is still growing." She paused, swallowed, then continued, "But the darkest rain clouds bring the brightest rainbows. I'm not giving up hope. Nobody is. All the doctors are working hard to find the right combination of treatments. All the nurses are pulling for him. Jake's a favorite on the oncology wing. How could he not be? He's such a sweetheart. So appreciative of everything that's being done. I mean, even when they're sticking him with needles and pumping him full of toxic medicine and he's barfing his guts out, he's still saying, 'Thanks for taking care of me.' He's a saint. A freaking saint."

Margie ran a hand through her damp hair. She pulled out the baby monitor she kept in her pocket. It was on. Of course it was. But she checked it compulsively when she was in the basement or when she had to go outside to take out the trash or mow the grass. At least she hadn't had to mow for a couple weeks. Everything had browned out in the heat. Sometimes when she looked at the brittle grass and withered plants surrounding the house, she felt like the foliage was tuned into Jake. As his light dimmed, so did everything else on the property.

She looked at the monitor again. She didn't want to miss it if Jake called out to her. Not that he did very often. He usually just waited until she was in the room to ask for what he needed. Once, she went in his room and found out he'd thrown up all over himself, but he hadn't called her.

"I knew you were in the basement. I didn't want to make you come up the stairs more than you have to already," he'd said.

A saint.

Margie turned on the recorder again. "I wish I'd started this when I first came here to work, but I only just got this phone and this app. I want to record everything I can remember about being with Jake and then keep up with daily stuff from now on." She sighed. "I never thought I'd work here this long. It was supposed to be a transitional job because I didn't get the internship I applied for, and I kind of needed to eat. Evan obviously was desperate to find someone to take care of Jake. And then, of course, I fell in love with this kiddo, and so . . . well, I can do my photography and drawing later, after he gets well." Margie tapped the pause button on her app. She'd heard the falseness in her voice when she said *after he gets well*. She was more worried than she'd admit.

She hit the record button again. "Jake has what he calls a 'Pine Nut.' It's actually his version of the acronym for what he has, PNET, which stands for primitive neuroectodermal tumor. That's a fancy name for a kind of brain tumor, and his specific kind of PNET is a pineoblastoma. When Evan explained all this to Jake, as best he could, Jake said, 'Cool. I have a Pine Nut.' He was barely six years old at the time. I don't think he thinks it's so cool now. He's had all the treatments they can throw at his kind of tumor, and nothing's working. His headaches and double vision are getting worse. They tried removing the tumor, but they couldn't get it all, and it grew back, and now it just keeps growing. I'm not giving up hope, but—" She pressed stop. She wasn't going to record what Jake's head neuro-oncologist said. *The odds are against him.* If she recorded it, she would make it real.

The washing machine thumped as it shifted from agitating the towels to draining the soapy water. Margie jumped up. She'd been down here too long. She'd get back to her recording later, after Jake was asleep.

"Batter up." Margie leaned over Jake and kissed his forehead.

Her lips were sticky with lip gloss, but Jake always waited until she was gone to wipe his forehead clean. Jake smiled at her and snuggled his bat closer to his side. The bat was a plush baseball bat named Bodie. Margie made it for him not long after she became his nanny.

Three years before, as soon as he'd announced he was too old for teddy bears, he'd regretted it. He really did love his teddy bear, but every time his dad called him "my little man," he felt like a baby for wanting to hang on to something at night. Somehow clutching a baseball bat, even though it was soft and fuzzy and had a goofy, googly-eyed face, was manlier than hugging a bear. Margie understood that.

Jake loved Bodie, but Bodie was smelling a little sour these days. Jake had only thrown up on Bodie once and

Margie had cleaned it, but Bodie was absorbing the smell of all the medicines in Jake's body. He could smell them in his sweat. He hated that.

"G'night, Margie," Jake said.

"Good night, sweetheart."

Jake closed his eyes.

He used to wait until she was out of the room to close his eyes, but now he closed them to try and get her to leave the room faster. This wasn't because he didn't like her. He loved her. But Simon wouldn't come if she was here.

Usually, the eye-closing thing worked. Tonight, it didn't. She didn't leave.

Jake hadn't told Margie that Simon would only visit after Jake's lights were off and he was going to sleep. Margie seemed to believe him when he told her about Simon. However, he thought she might not like it if she knew Simon only talked to him after Margie said good night and left.

Jake made himself breathe slowly and evenly so she'd think he was going to sleep. And still, she stayed. He knew she was watching him. She did that sometimes. She'd sit on the edge of his bed while she thought he was sleeping. He usually wasn't, but he'd pretend to be.

Jake wondered what she saw when she looked at him. Did she see what he saw when he got a glimpse of himself in the mirror—a bald kid with grayish skin, sunken cloudy green eyes, and dark circles haunting his cheekbones? He hadn't been able to see Jake, the real Jake, in a long time.

But he remembered that Jake. That Jake had a round freckled face, bright green eyes, a big smile, and a thick tangle of brown curls that were usually falling over his eyes.

The bed shifted, letting him know Margie was standing. He waited to hear his wood floor creak in that spot between the green rug under his bed and the door. When he heard that creak, he knew it would only be a few more minutes . . . just a few more minutes until Simon came.

Margie closed the door to Jake's room. He curled on his side and hugged Bodie. He waited.

While he waited, he counted. It only took seventeen counts before he heard the voice coming through the little cabinet door.

"Heya, Jake."

The first night Simon had talked to Jake, Simon had made it clear he would be in the cabinet until Jake got well enough to walk to the cabinet, open the door, and find him. "When you can do that, I'll be here waiting for you."

At first, Jake thought that was weird; but he didn't want Simon to leave, so he'd accepted it. Sometimes, he wondered why Simon had to talk to him from inside the cabinet, but he was just having so much fun talking with his friend that he'd forget to care about it.

"So what did you do today?" Simon asked.

Jake sighed. "It wasn't a great day. Usually two days after chemo, I do okay. But I threw up a—"

Simon made a *plrrb* sound. "No, what did the *real* Jake do today?"

"Oh yeah."

Jake wasn't sure why he often forgot Simon's rules. Jake wasn't supposed to talk about things the way they were. He was supposed to talk about things the way they'd be if he was a normal kid able to do normal things.

He grinned. "I played . . . oh, wait. I almost forgot! Would you like some crackers? I have some out here for you." Jake waved his hand toward the little plate of crackers sitting on his nightstand. A small glass of juice sat next to it. Margie had said, "Simon will need something to wash down the crackers."

"That's very nice of you, Jake," Simon said. "But no, thank you. I'll be in here until it's time for you to find me."

Jake realized he hadn't really thought through his idea to offer Simon something to eat. "I could push the crackers toward the door," he said.

Simon laughed. "That's okay. It's enough that you thought about giving me some. Makes me feel good. Thanks."

"Okay."

"Now, tell me what you did today."

"Oh, well, I played in the sprinkler today with my friends."

"Which friends?"

"The Henderson kids, you know, Patty and Davey and Vic. And the twins from across the street, Ellie and Evie, were there, and Kyle Clay, and Garrett from the street behind us. We were trying to see who could slide the farthest."

"You slid in the grass when it got really wet?"

Simon's voice, already a little higher than Jake's, went even higher. He sounded really excited. "I did that today, too!" Simon said. "And I got grass stains on my knees. They're still green!"

Jake laughed. "Mine too."

"Cool! What else did you do?"

"Well, before we ran in the sprinkler, we all played softball in the park. That's why it was so good to be in the sprinkler later. It was really hot in the park. I sweated like crazy."

"Was the ground really dry? It was really dry where I played, and so when I slid into first, I scuffed up my knee. You should see the marks!"

"I got some scrapes, too," Jake said. "They're not bad, though. It didn't hurt."

"Mine didn't hurt, either, but my knees feel like sandpaper. I think it's fun. My dad once said stuff like that is a badge of honor."

"Yeah. I like that." Jake smiled and reached for his perfectly smooth knee. He imagined that it felt rough. If he concentrated, he could make his fingers believe he had scrapes on his knees. He even could feel a little sting on his skin.

"So did you make it?"

"Make it where?"

"To first base, when you slid?"

Jake grinned. "Sure I did. Then I stole second, too!"

"Way to go! Then what happened?"

"I got to third on a deep fly ball."

"Super cool!"

"I started trying for home on the next fly ball, but it wasn't far enough, and Clay caught it easily. So I had to run back to third."

"Can of corn."

"What?"

"That's what my grandpa called those easy fly balls."

"How come?"

Simon laughed. "You always like to know why, right?"

"Sure." Jake would have looked it up on his tablet, but he had to keep his eyes closed.

"Yeah, I like to know why, too. So I asked my grandpa, and he said the 'can of corn' thing could have started in a couple ways. The first way was because of when they used to sell groceries in small stores with high shelves. The men who owned the stores—they were called grocers, Grandpa said—would use long poles to knock cans of vegetables off high shelves and catch them in their aprons. Corn was the most popular vegetable, so that's why it made its way into the saying."

"I think I saw one of those grocers in a Western movie once," Jake said.

"Yeah, me too! It was just like Grandpa said."

"So what's the other way?"

"The other . . . Oh yeah. Well, Grandpa said 'can of corn' could have started because many, many years ago, games were played in cornfields."

"That's cool."

"Yeah, but I think it would be way hard to find the ball under those big, tall corn plants. It would be like playing baseball and hide-and-seek at the same time."

Jake laughed. "That's funny."

Simon laughed, too. "So what finally happened? In the game?"

"Oh, um, well, Vic hit a double. So I ran home."

"Awesome!"

"It was fun."

"So what'd you do after the game?"

"Um . . . we went for ice cream."

"Mm, I love ice cream. What flavor did you get?"

"Chocolate. Duh."

Simon laughed. "I had chocolate ice cream today, too! And I ended up spilling some on my shirt. Did you do that?"

"Yeah, I did. Right on my shirt!"

"Sometimes chocolate stains don't come out in the wash. Oh well. If it doesn't, we'll remember that ice cream for a long time, right?"

"Yeah, I bet you're right," Jake said. He yawned.

"It sounds like you're tired. How about I come back tomorrow night?"

Jake wanted to say he could stay awake, but he really couldn't. "Okay. I'd like that."

"Me too. Good night, Jake."

"G'night."

★ ★ ★

Margie was awake the next morning when the phone rang. It was early, and she hoped Jake would sleep through the ring so she could surprise him.

"Hi, Evan," she said.

"Hi, Margie. How's my little man?"

"He's strong like his dad."

Evan laughed. "Flattery doesn't work on soldiers."

Margie grinned. "It was worth a try."

"He have a rough go of the chemo?"

"Yeah. One of the worst ones so far. I still don't understand why a medicine that's supposed to make him better makes him so much worse."

"Yeah . . . hopefully one day they'll find a better treatment."

Margie heard someone shout through the phone line. "Everything okay?"

"Sure. Guys letting off some steam."

"You ever do that, Evan?"

"What?"

"Let off steam."

"Me? No. Steam is pretty much what keeps me going."

Margie laughed.

"Is there anything you need to tell me?" Evan asked.

Margie remembered she had to stay on point so he'd be sure to have time to talk to Jake. You never knew when these calls could be cut short.

"I already emailed you about the chemo. So, no. You're up-to-date."

"And you?"

"What about me?"

"How are you holding up?"

"I'm fine. Well, I'm not fine, but I'm fine enough that I'd be thrilled to death if everyone else, namely you and Jake, were as fine as I am."

"Well, that's fine, then." Evan chuckled.

Margie laughed again. She loved that this man on the other side of the world, this man who was in a life-and-death situation pretty much every day, this man with the very sick son, this *widower*, this *soldier*, always managed to make her laugh.

Margie stood and headed toward Jake's room. "I assume you're ready to talk to him?" she said to Evan.

"Raring."

Margie pushed Jake's door open, and he lifted his head. She pointed at the phone in her hand. "It's your dad."

Jake pushed himself up and grinned. His eyes flashed a hint of their old brightness for just an instant before pain dimmed them again.

"Here's your little man," Margie said into the phone.

"You take care of you," Evan said.

She didn't respond. She handed the phone to Jake.

"Hi, Dad!"

Margie adjusted the pillows behind Jake so he could relax but still remain sitting more upright. She smiled at him when he said to his dad, "Yeah, Margie's been mean to me as usual. Really mean."

His laughter rang out as she left the room.

That night, Jake forgot again and tried to tell Simon about his conversation with his dad and his appointment with Dr. Bederman. And as usual, Simon said, "I want to hear about what the *real* Jake did today."

"Oh yeah, right." Jake wondered why he couldn't remember that. But he'd worry about that later.

"Today, my dad and I went to the movies," Jake said. He figured the real Jake would have a dad who was home to do things with him.

"Really? What did you go see?"

"It was a sci-fi movie, about robots."

"Ohhh, that sounds great! I went to the movies, too. I had popcorn. Did you have popcorn?"

"Yeah!"

"I bet you got butter all over your face, right? And on your clothes? And did you get some popcorn stuck in your teeth? I sure did."

"Yeah, I did. Right between my two front teeth."

"Cool. What else did you do today?"

"My friends and I built a fort out of sticks in the backyard."

"Same friends you played with yesterday?"

"Uh-huh. It was hot, and we needed more shade. So we *built* shade. I mean, not really. We built a fort, though."

"I love building forts. I built one, too. I got a splinter. Did you get a splinter?"

Jake felt his index finger and said, "Yeah, I did."

"I still have this little brown mark under my skin on the end of my finger from where I got a splinter once."

"Another badge of honor?"

"Yeah, exactly."

Margie stretched out on the twin bed nestled under the eaves in her cavelike room. She'd always wished she was taller than her five foot three inches, but ever since she'd started working for Evan, her size had served her. Evan's bungalow was small, with a living room, a tiny kitchen, two bedrooms, and a bath on the first floor; then there was an itsy-bitsy room with slanted ceilings upstairs on what Evan called the "half floor." He'd been using the room as an office, but he cleared it out and put in a twin bed, an almost-doll-size bureau, and a nightstand for Margie when she took the job. The furnishing was sparse, but the room had built-in shelves and cabinets. It also had a window that looked out on the upper branches of the apple trees in the backyard. One of the trees reached to within a foot of the window. The previous year, she'd been able to pluck an apple off the tree from her room. The trees made her feel as though she lived in a woodland tower like the cartoon princess Jake said she resembled.

Right now, most of the window was obscured by a pedestal fan blasting not nearly enough air into the little room.

Margie's hair blew over her forehead and stuck to her skin. She hated having the fan on high speed because it was almost as loud and droning as an engine. The sound made her nervous. She was afraid she wouldn't be able to hear Jake if he called out.

Margie picked up her phone and tapped the recording app. "Jake barely ate anything this evening. Just a couple of crackers. If I didn't know better, I'd think he hated my cooking." She laughed, but the sound was forced. "But I do know better. When I first came here, Jake couldn't get enough of my mac and cheese and my lasagna." She sighed. "But he hasn't had an appetite in a while."

Margie paused and listened. She stared at the baby monitor she'd set on her nightstand. It was toggled to high volume. Had Jake just made a sound? No. Nothing.

Margie set down her phone and ordered herself to go to sleep. She wondered if she'd comply for a change.

The next night, Jake told Simon about the pizza he and his friends had after they ran through the sprinkler again.

"I had pizza, too!" Simon said. "Did you get pizza sauce on your clothes and all over your face? I sure did!"

Jake laughed. "Yep. I think I still have some there." He thought he tasted tomatoes and garlic at the corner of his mouth. Wow. He was getting good at this imagining thing . . . because all he'd really had for dinner was a couple bites of scrambled egg and two bites of toast. He still felt bad about all the food he wasted. When he had said so to Margie, she'd said, "Oh, don't worry. I'll box it up and send it to needy kids."

That had made him laugh so hard he snorted. He could just imagine a package of scrambled eggs going through the mail.

"It would spoil," he'd said through his giggles.

"And that would be bad," Margie had said.

"Very, very bad," they'd said together.

"I tell you what," Margie had begun. "How about we send some of your allowance to a place that helps feed kids who need food? That make you feel better?"

Jake had felt a surge of excitement. "Yes!"

"Good deal," Margie had said.

"So what else did you do?" Simon asked. Jake immediately felt bad that he'd been thinking about Margie while Simon was here.

"Oh, um, well, after we had pizza, we went to the twins' house. They have air-conditioning, and we were all really hot."

"What did you do there?"

"We finger-painted. Can you believe it? I haven't done that since I was really little."

"Oh, I love finger-painting. All that cool, sloppy paint. I did that today, too. And I got a different color paint under every one of my fingernails. Did you do that? I bet you did!"

Jake smiled at the thought of a rainbow of colors under his nails. "Yes, I did that, too. Now my fingers are a rainbow."

"Yeah, exactly! Mine too!"

Jake was going to say something else about the paints, but instead, he yawned.

"You're getting tired?" Simon asked.

"A little."

"That's okay. I can leave so you can go to sleep. But hey, remember what I told you. When you're well enough to walk around and do stuff, *then* you can come open the cabinet door. I'll be here waiting for you when it's time. Okay?"

"Okay."

Margie stepped out onto the front porch to clear her head before she went to bed. Movement in the Hendersons' yard startled her, and she whirled to peer through the spotty light.

"Sorry," Gillian Henderson called softly. "It's just me."

Gillian stepped into the light cast by the front porch lamp. She was wearing a pale blue bathing suit under a darker blue T-shirt. And she was drenched.

Margie suddenly realized she could hear the measured spitting sound of the sprinkler in Gillian's yard. "Were you running through the sprinkler?"

Gillian grinned. Tall and broad-shouldered, Gillian had the weathered face and flyaway sun-bleached hair of a farmer's wife, even though she was married to an accountant. She once told Margie she got her rugged looks from running after half the neighborhood children. Because

Gillian was a stay-at-home mom with infinite patience, most of the kids tended to congregate at her house. And despite having a houseful of kids every day, Gillian was always asking Margie if there was anything she could do to help. Margie figured Gillian was at least fifteen years older than Margie, but they'd become good friends.

"Fun is not just for kids," Gillian said. "And I was so hot I was sure I was going to combust."

Margie laughed. "I hear you."

"When the kids are up, they don't want Mom in the sprinkler. 'It's *embarrassing*,'" she mimicked her daughter's voice.

"Are they at that age already?"

"I think mine were born at that age," Gillian said.

Margie laughed.

"Hey, you want to join me?"

Margie looked down at her T-shirt and shorts. "Why not?"

Then she hesitated. The baby monitor. She pulled it out of her pocket and looked at it. She couldn't get that wet.

Gillian saw Margie staring at the baby monitor. "Wait here." She trotted toward her house.

Margie listened to Gillian open and close her squeaky screen door. She watched a car go by, then looked up to try and find the Big Dipper. She spotted it seconds before she heard Gillian's screen door squeak again. She looked toward Gillian's two-story Craftsman. Gillian's house shared styling with Evan's, but hers was probably four times bigger.

Gillian jogged over. "Here." She handed Margie a zippered plastic bag. "You'll still be able to hear it, but it won't get wet."

"You're brilliant."

"I'm a mom. Working the problem is my specialty."

Margie dropped the baby monitor in the bag.

"Come on," Gillian said.

Margie let Gillian lead her into the adjacent yard, and the two women began running through the sprinkler like little girls. Back and forth, in and out, twirling and skipping—they played in the water and danced all over the soggy grass. Dirt squishing between her toes and water spraying in her face, Margie couldn't remember the last time she'd felt so light and free.

After nearly half an hour, they staggered to Evan's front porch and collapsed, dripping, on the steps. Margie realized her muscles were more relaxed than they'd been in months.

For several minutes, they breathed and dripped in silence. Then Margie started to cry.

Gillian put her arm around Margie and pulled her close. "It sucks," Gillian said. "It just sucks. He's a great kid."

"Yes," Margie said, "he is."

The next day, just before noon, someone knocked at Jake's window. Jake heard his name being called. He craned his neck to see around the fan.

The sun's rays speared through the window and advanced nearly all the way through the room. Sweat trickled down his spine.

"Jake? You in there?"

Grimacing, Jake pushed himself up. "Is that you, Brandon?"

"Yeah, it's me. I came to see if you wanted to break out?" Brandon's long face appeared just above the bottom of the window. The screen distorted his features.

"Oh . . . Brandon, I can't. I'm not supposed to even get up without help. I'm sure not supposed to go out."

"Yeah, but what if you wanted to?" Brandon pressed his face into the screen to squish his nose. He made silly faces at Jake.

Jake laughed. He looked toward his room's half-open door. He wasn't sure where Margie was, but he knew she was here someplace. If she had to leave the house, she got Mrs. Henderson to stay with Jake, and Mrs. Henderson always came in to give him a hello hug when she arrived. Margie didn't leave often, though. Mostly, she had things delivered to the house. If she went out, he went with her, because most of what she had to do was take him to doctors and to treatments.

"Come on, Jake. I haven't see you in forever," Brandon whined. "I miss you."

Jake looked toward the window again. Even through the screen, he could see Brandon's blond hair sticking straight up. He smiled. "I've missed you, too."

Brandon was Jake's best friend from school. They used to be inseparable.

For the first year after the doctors found Jake's Pine Nut, he went to school as much as he could, in spite of his headaches. Then he had brain surgery to try and get the tumor out. He was at home for several weeks, but he went back to school as soon as he could. The year before, he'd gone to school about half-time. Now, school wasn't possible at all. He was too weak and sick.

But maybe he could go out with Brandon. Wouldn't that be cool?

Jake was already dressed. He refused to sit around in bed in pajamas or underwear. Even on his worst days, he wanted to be dressed. So he had on green shorts and a tan T-shirt. He didn't have any shoes on, but he knew slip-on sandals were there, just under the bed. He could wear those.

"Are you coming?" Brandon asked. "I thought we could go to the arcade. If you're tired or weak, we can just do the racing games you sit down for."

Jake loved the racing games. Okay. He was going to go for it!

"All right. Give me a minute," Jake said.

"Okay." Brandon pulled back the corners of his mouth and stuck his tongue against the screen. Then he said, "I'll be out here melting. If you take too long, I might be a puddle, but I'll be here. Just scrape me into a bowl or something and we can go."

Jake laughed. "Okay."

He sat straight up and waited while the room settled around him. He blinked to be sure he could tell eye echoes from real things. He'd had double vision for so long, he'd learned to adapt, but sometimes, when he reached for something, like a sock, he'd reach for the sock that was the echo instead of the real sock.

Pretty sure he could tell what was real and what wasn't, Jake swung his legs over the side of the bed. All four of his pale legs were bony. "Come on," he encouraged them, "hold me up. I'm not that heavy."

His legs apparently disagreed because the first time he tried to stand, he fell back onto the mattress, barely. He nearly fell to the floor but caught himself on the side rail of his hospital bed.

When he'd first gotten the hospital bed, he'd been so upset. "I won't sleep in that! I'm not dying!" he'd yelled at Margie.

"Of course you're not," she'd said. "But you're a good kid, and you know that if something will make my life easier, you don't mind doing it."

When she'd put it that way, how could he refuse?

And now he was glad he had the bed. Using the side rails, he was able to prop himself upright while his legs remembered what it was like to stand on their own. He felt like a baby horse he'd seen once on TV. He was wobbling all over the place.

But horses stood, and so could he.

Jake concentrated, and he made himself stay upright even though his head started to pound and pressure built up behind his eyes. He looked down, spotted the sandals, and fished for them with his right foot. No way was he going to be able to lean over. That would put him on the floor for sure.

Bending his knee to move his right foot around made his knees almost give out—almost, but not quite. He was able to snag the right sandal and put it on. He then planted his weight on the sandal, which gave him more stability, and he began poking at the other sandal with his left toe. Eventually, he snagged that one, too.

From outside the window, Brandon called in a strangled cry, "I'm melting!"

"Shhh," Jake hissed. "Margie will hear you."

Brandon laughed.

Jake pushed away from the bed, letting go of the railing. His body swayed like a skinny tree in a big wind, but he didn't fall. He could do this.

"Oh, I forgot to tell you," Brandon said, reappearing at the window. "Hey, you're out of bed. Good job!"

"What did you forget to tell me?" Jake asked. He got up the nerve, and he took one stiff, hesitant step.

He almost fell again. He was beginning to think this wasn't a great idea.

"Oh, I forgot to tell you I brought my brother's wagon," Brandon called. "I thought you might need a ride to the arcade."

Well, that would make it easier for sure. Jake could make it to the window, and then Brandon could help him out and into the wagon. Then Brandon could pull him. The idea gave Jake a little more confidence. "Why didn't you say so?" he called out as he took another step. This time, he was a little steadier.

"The sun has melted my brain. It's running out of my ears."

"Ew."

"Yeah. Exactly. Hurry."

Jake took another step. He stayed up. He took another. He was still standing. One more. Still up. One more. He was clutching the windowsill, looking out at Brandon, who was pretending to sword fight an imaginary opponent, using a stick.

"Hey! There you are!" Brandon dropped the stick and hurried to the window.

"Here I am." Jake braced his hip against the windowsill and reached out to unseat the screen so he could push it out. His head went a little fuzzy, and the double screen got a little difficult to separate out. He managed it, though, and when he gave the screen what he thought was a real shove, Brandon lifted the screen out. Score!

"This is so awesome," Brandon said.

"Yeah," Jake agreed. "Okay, give me a second."

"Can I hold your arm or something?"

"Yeah. That would help." Jake managed to plant his butt on the ledge. Holding on to the window jamb with his left hand, he reached his right hand out through the open window. Brandon took his hand. "I've got you," he said.

Jake hoped that was true. Leaning back against the window jamb, he shifted his weight and swung his right leg through the window. He got a little too much momentum, and he almost threw his whole body through. But Brandon steadied him.

His headache got worse, and his stomach started to do flips. He tried to ignore both.

Concentrating, Jake was able to swing his other leg through the window. This time, he had a little more control.

"Okay, now just turn a little more and slide on out of the window," Brandon said. "I'll be sure you don't fall."

Jake paused and peered out at the world he saw so little of these days. It was bright, hot, and dry, just as it had been the last time he'd looked. A roasting breeze stirred the elm's branches, and they made scratching sounds against the house's brown siding. Jake heard the twins giggle across the street, and he suddenly felt giddy, like he was sneaking out of school. Not that he'd ever done that. But it also felt like looking for your presents before Christmas. He *had* done that. He'd found them, too, and then when Christmas came, it was a letdown because he already knew what he was getting. That was a lesson. Sometimes waiting was better.

"Are you coming the rest of the way?" Brandon asked.

"Oh. Yeah." Jake steadied himself in the open window, took a deep breath, and then slid out.

If Brandon hadn't been there, he'd have ended up a heap on the ground. But Brandon was true to his word. He caught Jake and held him up.

"You good?" Brandon said.

"I'm okay."

Brandon looked at Jake's face. He frowned. "Whoa. I didn't know."

"Know what?"

Brandon shook his head. "Nothing." He looked around. "If I help you to the tree, can you lean on it till I get the wagon over here?"

Jake saw the bright red wagon parked on the sidewalk. "Okay."

With Brandon holding him in a tight grip, Jake began to walk. But the nausea got worse. And his legs got weaker.

Suddenly, Jake collapsed and vomited all over the dry grass. Brandon jumped back just in time to avoid getting spewed on. Jake was glad for that. He didn't look up at his friend. He was too embarrassed. And he felt like he was used up, sort of like an empty toothpaste tube, all squeezed out and limp. How was he going to get back up?

The answer to his question came flying around the corner of the house. It was Margie, running to Jake, as if she knew he needed her.

"What in the big wide world are you doing?" Margie's voice was higher than Jake had ever heard.

Brandon took a couple more reverse steps, distancing himself from both the vomit and Margie's obvious upset.

Jake heard a screen door screech and slap, and Mrs. Henderson came running out of her house. "I just saw what was going on. What can I do?"

Brandon's eyes got really wide. He looked from Mrs. Henderson to Margie. He was suddenly as pale as Jake felt.

Margie bent over Jake. "Come on, you silly boy, let's move you just a little this way."

Mrs. Henderson joined them. "Let me help."

"Thanks," Margie said.

Together, the women lifted Jake and pulled him away from his mess, sitting him so his back was against the elm tree. Its bark felt rough through the thin material of his T-shirt. Jake pressed his hands against the tree's roots and held on to them. Mrs. Henderson squatted next to him. She brushed her fingers across his forehead.

Margie straightened and pointed a finger at Brandon. "You!"

Brandon winced.

Margie glanced at Jake and Mrs. Henderson. Then she took a deep breath and turned to Brandon. She lowered her voice. "I'm sure you meant well, but you need to go home. And don't try this again. He's not . . ." She cleared her throat. ". . . he's not well enough to go out right now."

"I'm sorry," Brandon said.

"I know. Now get." Margie softened her words with a half smile.

Brandon ran to the wagon and grabbed its handle. He ran down the sidewalk with the wagon rattling behind him. Jake watched until Brandon was out of sight. He was watching fun and freedom run out of his life.

Margie squatted next to Jake and Mrs. Henderson. "What were you thinking?"

"I thought I could be the real Jake."

Mrs. Henderson looked away. Margie twisted her mouth but didn't say anything. "You wait right here with Mrs. Henderson. I'm going to go get the wheelchair. Okay?"

"Okay."

"Promise?"

"Pinkie swear," Jake said.

Margie smiled and curled her pinkie finger around the one Jake extended. "You just aged me several years."

"So you're like, what? A hundred now?"

"Har de har," Margie said.

"That would make me two hundred," Mrs. Henderson said.

She and Jake laughed as Margie trotted toward the house.

Simon came as soon as Jake closed his eyes later that evening, even though he was going to sleep earlier than usual. His little failed adventure had drained him completely. Which sucked.

"Hi, Jake. Hot day today, huh? So what did you want to do today?" Simon asked.

"Brandon and I were going to go to the arcade," Jake said.

"You mean you *did* go to the arcade."

"Oh yeah. Yes, we went." Jake smiled as he curled up.

"And what did you do there?" Simon asked.

"We had so much fun," Jake said. "We played all the racing games. I love the racing games."

"I love those, too. I did one of those racing games today, too. And I won enough tickets to get a bunch of pencils. Did you win? I bet you won."

"We did. I got smiley-face erasers with my tickets."

"Oh yeah, those are fun. I got one of those, too! I like them because they cheer me up when I'm feeling down."

"You feel down?"

"Sometimes. Not very often, though. I'm too busy having fun!"

"Yeah. Me too."

"So hey, did you get a slushy at the arcade?" Simon asked. "I got one. I got grape. It turned my tongue purple. Did you get one?"

Jake laughed. He stuck out his tongue and imagined it was purple. "Yes! My tongue's purple, too!"

"Purple power!" Simon said.

"Purple power!" Jake repeated.

Jake couldn't believe how much he really felt like he'd gone to the arcade that day. He was sure he had. "Oh, we did that dance game, where you step on the lighted squares. Me and Brandon—we were bustin' a move!"

"I'm totally impressed, Jake! I mean, I'm pretty bad at those things. When I dance, I'm all like spastic and stuff."

Jake could hear clothes rustling and little breathy sounds coming from inside the cabinet, like Simon was doing a dance move right now.

"You know what's funny?" Simon asked.

"What?"

"I did that dance game, too, even though I'm a total spaz at it. I was so into it I stepped on my shoelace and ended up breaking it. Have you ever done that?"

"I did that today!"

"No! So you know what that is?"

"Badge of honor," Jake and Simon said in unison. Then they laughed together.

"What other games did you play today?" Simon asked.

"I played the shooting game, the one where you're shooting bad guys, like robbers and stuff? Brandon wanted to shoot aliens, but I don't like to shoot aliens. I like aliens. I wouldn't do the hunting one, either. I don't like shooting animals. I really like animals."

"I'm with you on that!"

Jake smiled. Thinking about the arcade games he liked made him forget about needing to see Simon.

"Were any of your other friends at the arcade?" Simon asked.

"Yeah," Jake said. "A few were."

"Did you play pinball?" Simon asked.

Margie sat on the floor, cross-legged, in the hallway outside of Jake's room. Her back was pressed against the wall.

The house smelled like the chocolate pudding she made
for Jake a couple hours before and the lemon polish she'd
rubbed on the hallway's wood trim that morning. Evan
didn't expect her to do things like polish woodwork, but
Jake was better off when the house stayed germ-free, and
she was better off when she kept moving, so when Jake
slept, she found things to do. The whole house was spotless
and shining.

Slumped against the glossy hardwood baseboard, Margie
let tears slide down her face. She didn't want to listen; it
felt like eavesdropping. But unless she put in earplugs, she
couldn't avoid hearing what Jake and his "visitor" were
saying. And she could never put in earplugs or use earphones
for that matter; she always needed to be able to hear Jake.

And so she listened as Jake told Simon that he wasn't the
best pinball player in the world but he liked to try.

"I do, too," Simon said.

Margie got a distorted stereo effect as she listened to
Simon's voice. It was coming through the door, muffled,
and it was also coming through the phone she held in her
right hand, which was positioned next to the backup baby
monitor she held in her left hand.

Margie felt a little like a magician, with the magic

secrets hidden behind a shimmering curtain. If Jake got out of bed and came into the hall, he'd see how the magic worked.

But he wouldn't get out of bed without Margie's help. The secret was safe.

It had been Evan's idea, and Margie thought it was brilliant.

Evan called Jake almost every day, and in the first few months after the tumor was found, Jake was receptive to his dad's positive encouragement. When Evan said, "Keep your chin up," Jake always said brightly, "I will." But when the surgery failed and Jake had to go through radiation and chemotherapy, he started getting sullen. For months, Evan tried to encourage Jake, and for months, Jake refused to accept the cheer.

Evan told Margie they needed some "magic." Jake needed to believe in someone who could pull him out of the horror that was his daily life and lead him into the joy of different possibilities. And that's how "Simon" was born.

Jake knew about the baby monitor that sat atop his chest of drawers. He didn't like it, but he knew it was there, and he accepted the need for it. He didn't, however, know about the backup monitor that was just inside the little white cabinet. That monitor was linked with the one Margie now held, and so it picked up and played Evan's disguised voice from inside the cabinet.

Evan, still overseas, was "Simon."

Evan decided Jake would be more responsive to

someone his own age. So Evan downloaded a voice distorter that turned his voice into a little kid's voice.

When Evan suggested the idea of becoming a little friend for Jake, a friend who lived in Jake's cabinet and only visited at bedtime, Margie wasn't sure Jake would listen to Simon any more than he listened to Evan, but she went along with it. She was willing to try anything.

But Jake did listen. He clearly loved the nightly visits. It made her smile when he closed his eyes right after she said good night; she knew he was trying to get her to leave the room faster.

"The more he imagines himself to be a normal little boy," Evan had told Margie, "the greater the odds he can be one again someday. He has to have hope."

Margie had agreed.

Jake started getting sleepy while Simon was talking about pinball machines, but he wanted to hear what Simon said.

"You know the secret to being really good at pinball?"

"What?" Jake asked.

"Nudge and tilt."

"What does that mean?"

"Well, some people think it's cheating, but I don't. It's like when you kind of shove at the machine, you know? With your hip or something? Sometimes when the flippers won't do what you want, you can save a ball with a little bump, sort of."

"I wish—" Jake stopped himself. He was about to say he

wished he could try that someday. Instead, he said, "I'm going to try that the next time Brandon and I go to the arcade."

"Yeah? Cool."

Jake yawned, loudly.

"I think you need to go to sleep," Simon said.

Jake mumbled, "Yeah, I think so, too."

"And remember," Simon said, "when you can walk again, come open the door to the cabinet. I'll be here waiting for you."

"I 'member," Jake said. And he fell asleep.

Margie quickly stood and walked away from Jake's door.

"How are you and Jake doing in the heat?" Evan asked when she put the phone to her ear.

Margie stepped into the living room and sat down on the small olive-green sectional under the front picture window. "I'm okay. I think it's draining him more, though. He's weaker than usual."

Margie had already told Evan about the aborted arcade trip. Evan was proud of Jake's attempt but relieved he hadn't made it far. "That could have been bad," he'd said.

"Very, very bad," Margie and Evan said together.

She grinned, thinking back to how that joke had started. Evan had wanted Jake to meet his uncle for the first time. Michael, Evan's brother and only living family, had lived in Europe for years, and he'd never met Jake or Jake's mom. Michael was back in the States, and Evan was taking Jake, and Margie, to meet him. The drive one way was several hours.

"Michael's a serious dude," Evan had warned Jake and Margie as they traveled. "He's, well, he's a little different. He's intense about making money, and he's really good at it. But the way he is about it, and, just the way he is, can make him seem like he's not human."

"So he's like a cyborg with bad programming?" Jake had asked.

They'd all laughed.

Just before they'd arrived at the hotel where Michael was staying, Jake had eaten a candy bar. No one thought much of it until Jake tried to hug his uncle. Michael, spotting the chocolatey fingers, had stepped out of Jake's reach. "You must exercise caution. You could get chocolate on my suit, and that would be bad. Very, very bad."

They had all had an awkward, stiff dinner together, and then they'd headed home. Driving down the freeway in the dark, Evan had said they should stop for gas or they'd run out.

"That would be bad," Margie had said.

And Jake had piped up from the back seat, saying, in a perfect imitation of his uncle, "Very, very bad."

Margie smiled at the memory.

"Margie? You there?" Evan's voice nudged through the phone.

"Sorry. I was thinking about that trip to meet Michael."

"Oh, that was bad."

"Very, very bad," they said again, in unison. They laughed. Margie wondered when that joke would get old.

"Speaking of Michael, I'll talk to him. I hate to ask him for favors, but I can't afford an air conditioner right now. I'll ask him to get one for Jake."

"Sometimes a soldier has to suck it up and take one for the team," Margie said.

Evan laughed. "You do that every day."

"What I do is a privilege," Margie said.

Evan was silent. Then he cleared his throat and said he had to go.

Now Margie leaned against Jake's door and listened to his even breathing coming through the baby monitor. Jake didn't snore, so it was challenging to know when he was deeply asleep. Once, when she was sure he'd gone to sleep, she'd opened the door to his room only to have him sit up and say, "What's wrong, Margie?"

She'd had to think fast. "I thought I heard you call out," she'd said.

Jake had accepted it. "You must have been dreaming," he'd said.

Tonight, though, when Margie opened the door, Jake didn't sit up. He kept breathing deeply, with long inhales and exhales. He was asleep.

But Margie still didn't move. She stood by the door with her eyes closed, listening to his breathing. Her closed eyes blocked out the evidence of Jake's illness. They erased the IV stand lurking in the corner of the room. Jake didn't need it right now, but sometimes, when he couldn't keep anything down, they had to hook him up to receive fluids and nutrients.

Her closed eyes removed the hospital bed and the line of prescription medication bottles marching across the top of the chest of drawers. They also transformed Jake's bald head back to the thick brown mess of hair that Margie could remember detangling when she first started taking care of Jake. He liked having his hair long, and Evan let him. "There's no law that says boys have to have short hair," Evan said. Margie thought that was funny coming from a man with a buzz cut.

Margie opened her eyes and adjusted to reality.

There was Jake curled up on his side, Bodie clenched against Jake's chest and belly, tucked under his chin. The pale yellow glow of the night-light put a shine on Jake's bald head and cast deeper-than-usual shadows under his eyes.

He was smiling in his sleep. That made Margie happy. She hoped he was playing at the arcade or running through the sprinklers.

Which reminded her . . . she needed to get to work.

Margie was three nights behind on her ongoing project. Two nights before, Jake's sleep had been unsettled. He kept waking up. Margie was sure it was caused by a change in dosage of one of his medications. Thankfully, Evan had arranged for her to have the authority to deal directly with the doctors about Jake's care. So she'd called Dr. Bederman and told him she was returning Jake to the original dosage. That did the trick, but then the next night, when he slept, she was so tired that she fell asleep and never got to her project.

When Margie first started working for Evan, she thought she was going to hate the sleeping arrangements—being stuck in that little room on the "half floor." She hadn't been looking for a live-in position. She'd liked her little apartment, and she was sure claustrophobia would do her in if she stayed here. But the position was full-time, with Evan being away so much. And over time, the house ended up charming her.

Chock-full of the wood trim and built-in shelving and cabinetry that were common in Craftsman homes, this house had even more character within its walls. Its original owner had obviously been fond of putting things out of sight, because the builder had put little hidey-holes in every room. He also had built funny little pieces of furniture specific to certain rooms, which had stayed with the house through the years. One of these pieces was the small white cabinet in Jake's room. Because Jake had plenty of storage in his closet and in other parts of his room, the cabinet had sat empty for years. Now, though, it had a purpose.

Margie's project waited for her in Jake's little cabinet, which was only a few feet from Jake's bed, just behind and to the left of the ugly green-plaid chair. Although she could take her project out of the cabinet and work on it in her room, it never seemed right to do that. Her project *lived* in the little cabinet. Moving it felt wrong.

Jake let out a deep sigh in his sleep, and Margie froze with her hand on the cabinet door. She breathed in and out, saddened by the astringent medicinal smells in the room. When Jake didn't move again, she grasped the knob and slowly pulled the door open.

Margie quietly sat down in front of the open door. She waited to be sure Jake was still sleeping deeply. Then she turned on the headlamp she wore. It was designed for crafters who wanted to see up close, and it suited Margie's needs perfectly. It allowed her to aim a small beam at her task without lighting up too much of the room. Jake usually slept hard, so there was little chance she'd wake him, but she didn't want to take chances.

In the glow of her headlamp, Margie's project looked at her with its simple hand-drawn eyes, one of which was blackened.

"Hi, cutie," Margie whispered.

Margie's project didn't respond. This was a good thing. Margie's project was a doll. If it had responded to her, she'd have shot up, whacked her head, and run for her life.

This doll was Evan's brainchild. Almost three feet high, plain white (at least originally), and now covered in evidence of the adventures Jake was having in his mind with Simon, Margie's project was an exercise in hope. Or maybe even more than hope. It was an exercise in belief.

If you were to infuse an object with enough love and

intention, would it have life? Evan apparently thought so, and maybe Margie did, too, now.

The white doll sitting in front of Margie was such an object. Born as simply a white-cloth doll with no face, no clothing, and no features or details of any kind, this doll now embodied the life of a healthy version of Jake. Weeks of "real Jake" experiences were drawn all over the doll. The blackened eye, for example, represented the day the real Jake stood up to a school bully. A drawn-on missing lower tooth represented the day the real Jake tried a tough trick with a skateboard. The doll's pockets were overflowing with drawings of tickets to movies and amusement parks and zoos. The doll's body was stained with the trials and tribulations of a joyful child's life. This doll was a reminder that the boy in question, although fading, was not gone yet. He still had enough imagination to conjure another adventure.

Margie set a zipper bag of colored markers on the green-carpeted floor and pulled a piece of paper from her jeans pocket. The paper held all the activities the real Jake had done over the previous three days. When Jake talked to Simon, Margie took notes.

Laying the paper on the floor next to the zipper bag, Margie pulled a thick brown marker from the bag. Nearly every detail on the doll had started with this marker. Sometimes, though, Margie needed to add color . . . like now. Putting a check mark next to *butter* on her list, Margie chose a pale yellow marker, too.

Concentrating, she drew a butter stain around the doll's mouth. Then she traded the pale yellow marker for the thick brown one and sketched part of a popcorn kernel between two teeth. It looked pretty realistic if she did say so herself. She knew her art degree would be good for something. Maybe she was missing her calling: She should have been a Real Kid Doll Decorator.

Margie grinned and looked at her list. Ah, the splinter.

Although Margie usually drew her additions to the doll, sometimes she used props. Like today. Reaching in her pocket, Margie pulled out a little plastic bag. Inside the bag were two splinters. One was maybe a half inch long. The other wasn't much more than a speck. She put one of the splinters on the pad of the doll's index finger, and she put the other splinter on the very tip of the doll's middle finger.

Margie looked at her list again. She checked off popcorn and splinters, and she moved on to pizza sauce. The doll already had a pizza sauce stain on its chin. Margie added another one at the corner of its mouth. She then rubbed a little garlic powder into the white cloth. She liked adding scents for realism when she could. Like the chocolate stain from a few nights ago. She'd used real chocolate for that, so the doll smelled chocolaty sweet.

Satisfied with the pizza stain, she moved on to the rainbow colors of finger paints under the nails. That was fun. She put a different color at the end of every one of the doll's fingers.

Then, using a black marker, she drew arcade tickets coming out of the doll's pockets. And once again, she used a prop when she glued a smiley-face eraser to the doll's hand. She'd thought that little tidbit was so important that she'd sent Gillian's daughter, Patty, to the arcade to win an eraser for her. It only cost Margie five dollars' worth of quarters to get it.

After she attached the eraser, she gave the doll a small tongue, and she colored purple stains on it. Then she studied the doll's feet. She'd never thought to draw shoes on the doll. But if she was going to draw a broken shoelace, there had to be shoes. So for the next several minutes, Margie bent over the doll's feet and drew green tennis shoes. Green was Jake's favorite color, and besides, green went with the grass stains on the doll's knees. The doll had a lot going on in the knee area—in addition to the grass stains, the knees had reddish scrapes and various hues of brown smudges from sliding into base on dirt and mud.

When Margie finished her work for the night, she sat back and studied the doll. It was turning into a hot mess with all the details she kept adding, but she knew that when Jake got to see it, he'd love it. It was intended to be a surprise for when he was well again. When he could walk, he'd go to the cabinet, open the door, find the doll, and he'd see all the things real Jake did while sick Jake concentrated on getting well.

Margie ignored the sharp twist in her intestines when she thought about Jake getting well. It was her inner compass telling her that Jake's recovery was by no means something Margie could expect. In fact, it was becoming less of a possibility every day.

"Stop it," Margie scolded herself in a whisper. "He's going to be fine."

She gathered her materials and stood. She made sure she closed the cabinet door before tiptoeing out of the room.

Jake tried to concentrate on totaling up the rent money he owed Margie for landing on her hotel-heavy property. He was having trouble counting the gazillion hotels she had, mostly because he was struggling to figure out which were the real hotels and which were the echo hotels. He had the same issue with the money. Which was the real money and which was the echo money? Of course, there was no "real" money, but Jake wished he could at least be sure about what was part of this world and what was being manufactured by his Pine Nut.

Well, no, that wasn't exactly right. His Pine Nut didn't make the echoes. Jake concentrated on remembering what Dr. Bederman had told him. Right. Dr. Bederman had said that because Jake's tumor was close to the nuclei that were in charge of eye movements, the tumor pushed in places where it shouldn't. So it was the nuclei that made Jake see double.

Jake had to look up *nuclei* to understand what Dr. Bederman was saying. He found out that *nuclei* was the plural form of *nucleus*. So he looked up *nucleus*, and he discovered that a nucleus was a little group of neurons in the central nervous system. Of course, then he had to look up *neurons* and *central nervous system*. He found out that a nucleus was a nerve cell, an "electrically excitable" cell. That made him laugh. He could imagine a little cell plugging into electricity and dancing all around like crazy. The central nervous system, he learned, was the combination of the brain and spine and all the nerves that made it so that humans could move and feel and think.

So basically, this little group of excitable cells was getting too crazy, and while they were partying, they were bothering Jake's eye cells. Seemed kind of rude to him, and he wished his nuclei would calm down. He was tired of seeing double.

Jake returned his attention to counting, but he realized he'd made a mistake. He had to start over. He didn't want to start over!

Grunting, Jake reached out and flipped the game board off his bed, sending fake money and echoes of fake money flying through the air, along with houses, hotels, and little playing pieces. The tiny dog almost hit Margie in the eye, and she said, "Hey!"

Jake immediately felt bad, but then he was angry that he felt bad. So he screamed.

He screamed at the top of his lungs.

And Margie didn't stop him. All she did was get up and step over to close his bedroom window.

The closing window did stop him, though. "Why'd you close it? Are you afraid people will think you're murdering me?"

Margie looked at him and rolled her eyes. "As if. Kiddo, if I wanted to, I could end you so quickly you'd never make a sound."

Jake's eyes got big, and Margie erupted into a clumsy ninja pose. She shouted, "Aaiiiyah!!" and pretended to kick toward Jake's bed.

That made him laugh. When Margie dropped her foot, stepped on another game piece and started hopping around the room, Jake laughed even harder.

"Sure, mock my pain," she said.

Jake kept laughing.

Margie stopped hopping around and went back to the window. "It's hot in here! Who closed the window?"

Jake giggled. "You did."

"Oh, did I?"

"Yeah."

"I'll take your word for it." Margie began cleaning up the game. "I assume you're done with this one for now?" she asked, as if it was normal to throw a tantrum over some stupid board game.

"I'm sorry," Jake said. "I got frustrated."

"Nooooo," Margie said in pretend disbelief. "You don't say? I just figured your wires got crossed or your circuits were frying."

Jake laughed again.

Margie grinned at him and returned to picking up fake money, game pieces, and tiny hotels and houses.

"I love you, Margie," Jake said.

Margie stopped moving.

She was bent over, her face turned away from Jake. It took a couple seconds, but she finally straightened and looked at him. Her eyes were moist. "I love you, too, Jake."

Margie sat on the front porch swing in the dark. She'd finished her daily project. Jake was sleeping restlessly. She had the baby monitor in her pocket as usual.

It was too hot in her little room to sleep. She'd tried sleeping on the sofa, but her thoughts wouldn't turn off. So here she was, using her foot to rock herself back and forth in the hopes that the soothing motion would relax her.

The sky was filled with stars, muted somewhat by the city lights in the distance. A couple fireflies darted in and out of the drooping boxwood at the corner of the house. Crickets chirped. The sound of oldies music and a TV show with a lot of shooting wafted across the street from open windows.

The air smelled dusty and stale. Summer had gotten old. Everyone was counting the days until fall brought cooling breezes and the relief of steady rain.

Would Jake make it to fall?

Margie groaned and rocked the porch swing faster.

Her days were getting harder. Not only was Jake's

double vision becoming more intense, his headaches were worsening, too. Increases in painkiller dosages made him weaker. His last two rounds of chemotherapy hit him hard. But that wasn't the worst part. The worst part was that Dr. Bederman had announced that the oncology team was stopping treatment.

"We don't have anything else," he told Margie after Jake's last round of chemo. "All we can do is manage his symptoms. If it gets to be too much for you, we can move him to hospice."

"He's not too much," Margie said.

Dr. Bederman nodded and patted her hand. "I understand."

Did he? Margie wondered. She was "just the nanny." She'd heard one of the nurses say that the previous week. Someone had asked the nurse if she was Jake's mom, and the nurse had said, "No. The mom's dead. She's just the nanny."

Sometimes, Margie wished she was like one of the robots Jake liked so much. Then she could be "just the nanny." She'd have no bothersome feelings to deal with.

But she wasn't just a nanny. She'd started that way, yes, but she'd lived with Jake for three years. She'd spent enough time with him that she knew him like a son, even back when he was well, before he became the invalid he refused to be.

She'd come to love Evan, too . . . not in any romantic way, more like a brother. When he was home on leave, he gave Margie the option to go on vacation, but she had no place she wanted to be for more than a few days. A couple times, she'd gone home to visit her parents and some old friends while Evan was home. Gillian had helped Evan out when Margie was away. But Margie wasn't gone long. So the three of them became like a little family, and she was included in the outings, the movie nights, the game nights, and the storytelling time. Then, of course, when Evan was overseas, she became Jake's whole world. And now *he* was her whole world, and even she couldn't muster enough positivity to convince herself her world was going to continue to spin on its axis.

Margie's parents wanted her to come back home. "You're going to be crushed when that boy dies. You should get out now while you can," her dad said to her.

Leave it to a retired marine to excise the emotion from the equation. Like she could drop Jake's failing body in a hospice center, pack up her few things, leave, and forget she ever heard of a boy named Jake. Just the thought made her so angry she wanted to climb through the phone line and strangle her dad.

"What happened to leave no man behind, Dad?"

"Why do you think I want you to get out?" he said. "I'm trying to bring you home whole."

"It's too late for that."

Margie just had to deal with it, like she always had.

But then the call came.

* * *

Margie and Gillian were making chocolate chip cookies. It wasn't a good day for chocolate chip cookies because it was so hot they probably could have fried the cookies in the street, but Jake had asked for homemade chocolate chip cookies, and Margie wasn't going to say no.

So Margie and Gillian were sweating together in the little kitchen. Margie had told Gillian she didn't have to help, but Gillian insisted. She said she might sweat off a pound or two, but Margie knew Gillian was there to offer moral support.

It was a good thing she was there.

For as long as Margie had worked for Evan, she knew "the call" was a possibility. Even so, she never expected it. She was so caught up in Jake that she tended to forget about Evan's precarious world.

So when it came, she wasn't prepared. Especially since it came from Michael.

"Margie," Michael said when she answered the phone. His flat, gruff voice was unmistakable.

"Hi, Michael."

"I have been notified that Evan's dead."

Margie's legs failed her. If Gillian hadn't been in the kitchen with her, she would have whacked her head on the counter as she went down. Instead, she fell into Gillian, who, though sturdy, was a lot softer than a counter. Gillian immediately wrapped her arms around Margie and propped her up.

"Apparently an IED hit the vehicle he was in," Michael said.

Margie gripped the phone and tried to breathe. She'd only met Michael the one time, and she knew the way he processed the world was very different from what was "normal," but hearing the news this way was—

"You there?" Michael asked.

She tried to speak, couldn't. She cleared her throat. "Here."

"I've got Evan's will here. He named you Jake's guardian, and he left you the house and some savings. I'm the executor. I'll follow the proper procedures and file what must be filed, and I'll bring you papers to sign when they're ready."

Margie couldn't find a word in her brain that made sense. Gillian took the phone from her hand.

Margie's voice didn't work again for an hour. Gillian filled in the gap. While Margie sat in a hard ladder-back chair at the oak pedestal table near the kitchen, Gillian coaxed more details out of Michael, checked on Jake, got Margie a glass of water, finished the cookies, and brought a load of laundry up from the basement to fold. Gillian didn't start to cry until she began folding Jake's T-shirts into neat little squares. Margie had been crying off and on the whole time.

After the laundry was stacked, the women sat together, holding hands and staring at the table. Margie's mind was blank. Well, not completely blank. She was trying to figure out how to get her tongue to work in concert with her throat and her gums again.

Eventually, she found her voice. "I'm not crying about Evan," Margie said.

Gillian looked up and nodded. "I know."

Margie wiped her eyes. "That sounds awful, though. I mean, I'm devastated that he's gone, of course." She sniffled.

Gillian pushed a box of tissues closer to Margie, who ignored it and wiped her nose with the back of her hand. "It's Jake I'm upset about." Margie dropped her face into her hands. "How am I going to tell him?" Her words, muffled by her palms, were as mushy as her thoughts.

Gillian put her hand on Margie's shoulder.

Margie looked up. "His oncology team doesn't think he has much longer," she whispered, as if saying the words in a normal tone would hasten their truth into being.

Gillian pressed her lips together, and her eyes filled. "I've known Jake since he was a tyke." Her voice was broken. She cleared her throat. "Evan and Roxanne moved in here when Jake was two. Even then, he was creative and kind." She smiled. "I love my kids, but they're oafs by comparison. It breaks my heart . . ." She shook her head and smacked the table. "But it doesn't do any good to try and figure it out or lament what is. All we can do is go forward from here."

Margie nodded, wanting to do pretty much anything but go forward from here.

"So I'm going to fix some lemonade," Gillian said. "We're going to drink it, and then you'll figure out the best time to tell Jake."

Margie nodded again. She felt like she was outside of herself, watching her body do things like nod and sit and fold laundry. She felt separate from this ordinary self. Getting the news about Evan had untethered her from day-to-day concerns.

"It's good Michael will handle Evan's estate." Gillian cut into a lemon. The tart scent filled the room, and it lured Margie partway back into her body. "I've never met Michael. He seemed a little, well, cool on the phone."

"He's a numbers genius, manages money for wealthy people and has made a killing doing it." She wiped her face. "He's not a bad guy. He just doesn't know how to connect. He doesn't feel the way we do."

"I might envy him," Gillian said.

"Me too."

"The shy robot knew he had to speak up about the glitch. If he didn't, the ship would crash. But he couldn't find his voice. All he could do was make little beeping sounds." Margie cleared her throat and then used a very squeaky voice to say, "Bleep. Blippity bleep bleep. Bloopity blip, blip bloooop."

Jake tried to smile because he knew it was supposed to be funny, but smiling took more energy than he had. Jake was only half listening to Margie's story. In spite of her attempts to get him "comfy" again, he was feeling so *not* comfy that listening was hard, and the story wasn't great, either. Usually, Margie told awesome stories, exciting stories filled with interesting characters doing cool things. But tonight, Margie's characters were boring. The "shy robot" was kind of stupid. Not that he'd tell her that, of course.

But he could tell her he was tired, so he did.

Margie frowned and leaned toward Jake. She tilted her head to study his face. Then she picked up his wrist to check his pulse. Her skin was sweaty, and her hair clung to her neck and the sides of her cheeks even though the fan tried to blow it around.

Jake thought of the fan as a knight battling a dragon spewing hot fire breath over everything in the room. Tonight, the knight was losing, big-time.

Margie let go of Jake's wrist and fussed over his IV line. A nurse had come that morning to put it in because he couldn't keep food down. The needle in the back of his hand pinched and stung. He hated it, but he didn't complain. He also didn't complain about the catheter. He hated it even more than the IV, but he was too weak to take care of things himself, and he was way too old to wet the bed.

"What can I get for you?" Margie asked.

"Nothing. I just want to go to sleep."

Margie chewed on her lower lip for a second, then nodded and handed him Bodie. Even though Jake knew Bodie would make him feel hotter, he gathered his plush bat close.

It wasn't true that he wanted to go to sleep. What he wanted was Simon. He was really excited about talking to Simon tonight because he'd thought of some cool things he "did" today. It had been so hot all day it had felt like the air wasn't even air anymore. It was lava flowing around the room, choking whatever it touched. Jake was having trouble breathing.

But even though he was lying in his bed too weak to do more than lift his hand, he decided that he wanted to be on the beach. If he was on the beach in heat like this, he could jump into the ocean and cool off. Maybe he could body surf or even learn to surf for real. He couldn't wait to tell Simon that he did that!

Margie bent over Jake and kissed his forehead. Her breath smelled funny. On the surface, it smelled like lemonade, but under that good smell was something bad, something kind of like vomit . . . or maybe that was his own breath he was smelling? He'd thrown up that icky yellow stuff a couple times this afternoon.

Jake closed his eyes, and as usual, Margie didn't leave the room. She stood by his bed and watched him. He kept his eyes closed and waited.

Once, he heard a faint shuffle, and he opened one eye a slit to see if Margie had moved. She hadn't. She'd just shifted position.

What seemed like several minutes went by. He thought he heard a sob, and he was tempted to open his eyes and look at Margie. But he remained still.

"Jake?"

He opened his eyes. Margie had never spoken to him after he closed his eyes.

"What?"

"I don't think Simon is going to visit tonight."

Jake blinked at her. "How do you know Simon visits at bedtime?"

Margie winked at him. He was sure the wink was supposed to be cheerful, but it looked wrong, kind of twisted and out of place. "I'm that good, kiddo." Her words didn't sound right, either. The usual lilt in her voice had been flattened by something Jake couldn't understand.

"No, seriously." Jake wasn't in the mood to be teased, especially when the teasing wasn't even done right.

Margie sat on the edge of the bed. "I've heard you talking to him through the door," she admitted.

"You were listening?"

"It's my job to be sure you're okay. When I hear something going on in your room, I have to check it out."

Jake thought about that. It was fine, he decided. It's not like he was telling Simon secrets. He didn't mind Margie knowing all the fun stuff the real Jake had been doing.

He frowned. "But why isn't he coming tonight?"

Margie blinked several times and swallowed. "Well, he just . . . he just can't tonight. You know how sometimes you're just not up to doing things you want to do?"

Jake nodded.

"It's like that."

Jake rubbed his eyes so they wouldn't give away how upset he was. For some reason, he didn't want Margie to know he was disappointed.

"It's okay," he told Margie.

She nodded. "Are you sure you don't want me to finish the story?"

He shook his head and closed his eyes again. "I'll just go to sleep."

She leaned over and kissed him again. Her cheek touched his; hers was wet.

Margie barely made it to Jake's door before her legs gave out. She quickly pulled the door shut behind her, and she slid down the wall to the floor, landing like a rag doll, her legs splayed out on the hardwood. Her sweaty skin squeaked against the wood polish.

The tears she'd tried to hold back in Jake's room, the ones that had started to slip down her cheeks in spite of her determination that they wouldn't fall, now wanted to burst from her like reservoir water freed of its dam. But she didn't let them. If she cried like she wanted to cry, Jake would hear her. She was not going to let Jake hear her cry!

So she gave in to some silent sobs, her shoulders heaving. Then, grasping her hair in both hands, she just sat and rocked herself. Margie had no idea how long it took, but eventually she felt settled enough and strong enough to get off the floor. Pressing back against the wall, she leveraged herself to a standing position. Pausing for an instant to listen to the baby monitor, she started down the hall toward the bathroom. But she ended up stopping outside of Evan's door.

She looked at the doorknob. Then she put her hand on it.

She never went in Evan's room while he was gone. When he was home, she'd go in the room to vacuum or put away laundry or whatever. When he was gone, though, coming in here felt like an invasion of privacy.

Now he was *gone*. And this house was hers. She still couldn't believe that.

Evan's room would be her room.

He'd wanted her to take it from the beginning. "It makes sense," he said. "You'd be right here next to Jake, and the bed's bigger, and it's cooler in the summer."

Yeah, and I'd feel like I was sleeping in your bed, she thought. "No, thanks. I need my own space," she told him.

She didn't realize until Michael gave her the news that the real issue was she wanted Evan to be more than just a boss, and being in his room when he was gone made her feel a little like a lovelorn stalker.

Love him like a brother. She snorted. Boy, had she been lying to herself.

Margie opened the door and stepped into Evan's room. It was just as she remembered it. Filled with cherry Mission-style furniture and dark green and light tan curtains and comforter, the room felt discretely masculine. Neat but not too neat, the room revealed its occupant. The walls were covered in family photos. Jake's happy and then not-as-happy face dominated those. The shelves were stuffed with fiction ranging from paperback mysteries to hardcover classics, nonfiction in dozens of genres, and how-to books revealing the ins and outs of doing everything from rebuilding a car engine to planting a garden. Obviously, Jake had gotten his insatiable desire for knowledge from his dad.

Crossing to the queen-size bed, Margie inhaled the slightly musty scent of the room. She was going to need to air it out.

She sat down on the edge of the bed. And she immediately shot up. It was too soon. She couldn't be in here.

Margie fled the room, shut the door, and strode into the bathroom. Inside, she shut the door, then blew her nose several times. She turned on the tap, ran cold water, and splashed her face.

When she wiped off her face, she braved a look in the mirror. Bad move. Her makeup was smeared. That meant it was on the towel. She looked down. Yep. Brown and black smudges streaked the tan terry cloth. Reaching into the medicine cabinet, Margie got out makeup remover and wiped her face clean. Then she gathered up the towels. She might as well do a load. She wasn't going to sleep anytime soon.

Margie sat up in bed. *What was that?*

In a testament to how little she knew herself, Margie had fallen asleep in the basement lawn chair while the towels were washing. So once she'd put the towels in the dryer, she went up to bed. Wearing just an exercise bra and shorts, she'd lain down on top of the covers on her bed. Her fan was aimed directly at her, but all its warm air could do was tickle the tiny hairs on her arms. Margie had closed her eyes and surrendered to the oppressive oven that was her room. She'd fallen asleep almost instantly.

But now she was awake again. Had she heard something?

Yes. Voices. She could hear voices.

Light from the outdoor lamp and a three-quarter moon spilled into her room through the open window above her bed. It was enough to illuminate the surface of her nightstand.

Where was the baby monitor?

Maggie took a breath. She'd left it in the basement.

Leaping out of bed, Margie left her room and padded down the steps to the first floor. Once there, she stopped. She could still hear the voices, but they were barely more than murmurs. She couldn't make out words. She couldn't identify the voices, either. Were they male? Female?

Was it Jake? If so, who was talking to him?

Instead of going down to the basement to get the baby monitor, Margie went toward Jake's room. The hallway was dark, but she could feel her way.

Running her hand along the top of the dark wainscoting trim in the hall, she listened as she approached Jake's room. She thought the voices were getting louder, but when she reached Jake's door, the voices went silent.

Margie stood perfectly still, listening.

Inside Jake's room, his fan hummed in undulating shifts from low pitch to high pitch. In the kitchen, the fridge added its voice to the throbbing motor chorus, and even farther away, Margie's fan contributed a deeper drone. Outside, a dog barked. Inside, the house made a cracking sound, like it was popping its knuckles . . . as if houses had knuckles to pop.

It had taken Margie a long time to get used to the bungalow's constant rasps and groans. On dark winter nights, she sometimes wondered if the house was alive. It sounded like it was uncomfortable and was trying constantly to shift into a better position. In the summer, it seemed more content, but it occasionally made some inexplicable sound that froze Margie in her tracks.

But sounds were sounds. Voices were voices. And Margie was no longer hearing voices.

She put her hand on Jake's door, tempted to open it and go in. She knew, though, that her night checks often disturbed him. If he was sleeping, she didn't want to wake him.

So Margie got the baby monitor and went back to bed.

When Margie checked on Jake early the next morning, she knew she could no longer put off what she'd been avoiding.

"Hi, Margie," Jake whispered when he saw her. His eyes were barely open. His skin was an almost translucent gray, and it was stretched so taut on his face Margie could see the perfect contours of his facial bones and his skull. He looked far more like a corpse than Margie wanted to admit.

"Hey, kiddo." She checked him over, bustling around the bed like it was a normal day and they were going to do normal things.

"So you'll never guess the forecast," Margie said.

"Um, hot?"

"Oh, you guessed! You're so smart!"

Jake did his best to smile. She watched him touch his tongue to a couple small cracks on his lips. It obviously hurt him to move his mouth.

Margie picked up a tube of lip moisturizer from the nightstand and gently applied some to Jake's lips. "What shall we do first today? Fly to the moon or build a spaceship?"

"You're silly," Jake said.

"I've been called worse." Margie snapped her fingers. "I know. We'll build a robot first. Then *he* can build the spaceship and fly us to the moon."

"Margie?"

Margie stopped moving. She looked at him, frowned, then sat on the bed. "What, Jake?"

"I don't want to pretend today."

Margie took a deep breath. She picked up Jake's bony, limp hand. "Okay. I won't make you. I don't want you to get mad."

"Okay."

"That would be bad," Margie said.

"Very, very bad," they said together.

Then Jake drifted back to sleep.

★　★　★

Wearing an old gray blouse she hadn't put on in years, Margie sat at the dining room table and methodically cut up every one of her smiley-face T-shirts. *Chrr, snip, chrr, snip* . . . the sound of the scissors sliding through the fabric and then snapping closed was surprisingly satisfying. Margie lost herself in her task. She cut steadily. Even when Margie's hand muscles started aching, she kept cutting. When she slashed her last happy yellow countenance, she dropped its remains in the pile and carefully placed the scissors next to it.

That's when Gillian showed up at the door, as if she knew Margie was going to need support to do what she had to do.

Stepping into the living room, Margie motioned for Gillian to come in. As soon as she did, Margie's tears returned, and Gillian strode to her. She took Margie's hand and squeezed it. Her chin moved against the top of Margie's head as she chewed gum. Margie smelled wintergreen.

"You can do whatever you have to do," Gillian said.

Could she? Margie wasn't so sure.

"The kids have gone on a day trip with friends," Gillian said. "Dave's at work. I'm here. What do we need to do?"

"It's time to call the hospital and arrange for Jake to be taken to the hospice center."

Gillian's eyes moistened, but she brushed her hands together and said, "Then let's go sit down and do that."

Gillian thought the process was going to be compli-cated, but Dr. Bederman had paved the way for Jake's transfer. All the paperwork was done. They just needed to send an ambulance with a couple EMTs and a hospice nurse.

"We can have the ambulance there by noon," the administrator told Margie.

"Thank you," she said, not feeling thankful at all.

She felt resentful. Angry. Enraged.

How could all the love and caring and positive expectations have brought Jake here? Margie had been so sure she could get him through this.

Outside, an ice-cream truck went by. The tinkling music sounded strangely ominous.

The ambulance arrived at 11:32. Margie's stomach roiled when she saw it pull up. She couldn't remember the last time she'd dreaded something as much as she dreaded this.

Margie had been checking the baby monitor regularly since she'd made the call. She hadn't heard anything. She'd looked in once to find Jake curled on his side with Bodie, his shoulders moving unsteadily up and down with his irregular breathing. She'd thought then about going in to tell him what was going to happen, but she couldn't bring herself to do it.

There was so much that she needed to tell Jake. First, of course, she needed to tell him that his father had died. Second, given that his father was dead, she thought she should reveal to Jake the identity of his nightly visitor. Wouldn't it be more comforting to know that his dad loved him so much he orchestrated those visits than it would be to believe in some nameless faceless friend who lived in a cabinet? Third, she had to tell him where he was going.

She'd planned on doing all of this before the ambulance arrived, but now it was too late. Okay, so she'd get him settled in hospice before she told him anything else.

Margie was pacing in the living room when the ambulance turned into the driveway. Gillian sat in the easy chair near the front door, her hands folded in her lap, her eyes closed.

For the first ten minutes after Margie had made her call, Gillian had tried conversation. She'd attempted to get Margie to talk about how she felt. But Margie wasn't ready to do that, and Gillian had correctly interpreted the monosyllabic answers as a plea for silence. Still, she stayed. Margie was grateful for that. She didn't want to talk, but that didn't mean she was strong enough to do what she was doing by herself.

"I'll get the door," Gillian said as two young blond EMTs and one dark-haired, middle-aged hospice nurse got out of the ambulance. The EMTs lifted a stretcher from the back of the ambulance while the hospice nurse approached the front door. She carried a clipboard and a medicine bag.

Gillian opened the door for the nurse. "I'm Gillian, friend and neighbor. This is Margie. She's Jake's nan—uh, guardian."

The short woman with a kind, round face held out her

hand. Margie managed to shake it, but she didn't say any-thing. What was she supposed to say? *Thank you for coming?*

"I'm Nancy," the woman said. She smiled at both Gillian and Margie. She was clearly an experienced hos-pice nurse; her smile was just big enough to be friendly but reserved enough to give deference to the situation.

"I have a couple things for you to sign," Nancy said to Margie.

The EMTs threw open the screen door and rolled the stretcher through. Its wheels clattered across the threshold, and Margie felt like the house was being invaded by armed intruders. She wanted to fight them off and force them to go away, which was ridiculous, because she'd called them.

"Just a sec, boys." Nancy held out her clipboard to Margie. "Sign here and here, for admission and to acknowl-edge that we'll be providing palliative care only. Then we can get Jake transferred and settled in."

Margie signed the papers, keeping her mind as blank as possible. But it wasn't blank enough. She felt like she was signing a piece of paper confessing to her complete and total failure as a caregiver, maybe even as a human being.

"All right, then." Nancy put the forms back on the clip-board. "That was easy enough. Let's go see Jake, shall we?"

Margie's muscles tightened. Gillian obviously sensed it, because she reached down and took Margie's hand, helping her out of the chair. "You're doing the right thing," she whispered in Margie's ear when Margie stood.

"This way," Gillian said to the EMTs. She led Margie through the living room and down the hall, stopping in front of Jake's door. She glanced at Margie and waited.

Margie opened Jake's door.

The second that Margie stepped into the room, she knew. She felt it.

The room was too still, too empty, even though Jake's poor depleted body lay in the bed. Jake was gone.

Because Margie turned into a statue in the doorway, Gillian had to practically lift Margie and move her aside to allow the EMTs and Nancy to enter the room. Gillian didn't say anything. Margie was pretty sure Gillian knew Jake was gone, too.

Nancy must have sensed it as well, because she frowned. Then she strode to the bed and felt Jake's pulse. She looked up at the EMTs and gave them a slight head shake. They stopped wheeling the stretcher, and they both stared at the floor.

Nancy looked up at Margie. "I'm so sorry. He's passed on."

Margie nodded. For once, her eyes were dry. What she was feeling was too much for ordinary tears. What she was feeling called for a screaming fit or a total mental breakdown. Since now wasn't the time for either of those, she had no response to offer. She was a human void. She wanted to fold into herself and fall into that void. She wanted to let it suck her from this room, from this reality. But she knew she couldn't escape so easily.

So Margie forced her legs to work, and she crossed to

Jake's bed. His body looked so small and fragile. She leaned over him and pressed her lips to his forehead. "I love you, Jake. I love you so much."

Bodie tickled her chin.

Gillian came up behind Margie and whispered, "Good-bye, Jake."

The three medical professionals wouldn't have had reason to see anything amiss. For all they knew, it was normal. Even Gillian would not have commented on it. She might have seen it, but she wouldn't attach any meaning to it.

Margie, though? Margie would have. But she didn't see. Nobody saw.

Five people. Five sets of eyes.

And none of them noticed the little cabinet door was wide open.

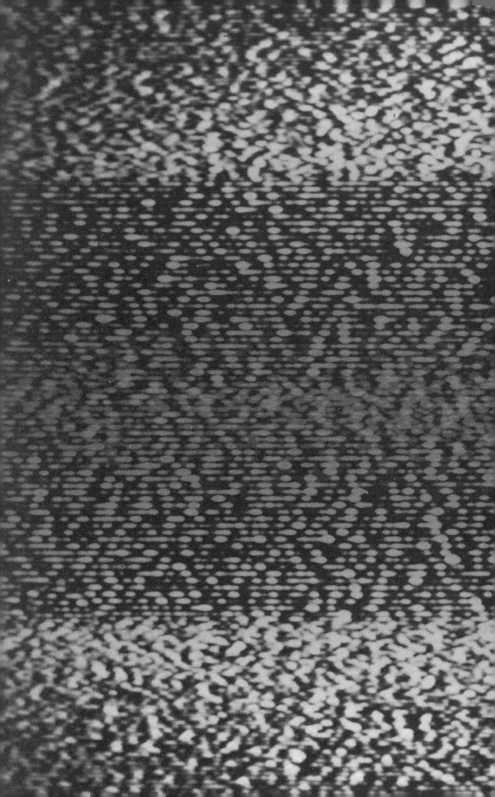

*T*oby! Toby! Toby!"

Kids chanted as Toby Billings hunched over the *Ultimate Battle Warrior* arcade game at Freddy Fazbear's Pizza and Games. His left hand clenched the joystick tightly, shifting left and right. Up and down. His right hand punched the action buttons for his warrior character to bust the graveyard ghoul opponent in the face and kick him in the gut. Repeatedly. Black blood and green sweat splattered from the ghoul.

It was freaking awesome.

Sweat dampened Toby's upper lip. He shifted the peppermint-flavored toothpick inside his mouth from one cheek to the other. His arm muscles clenched tightly. He was about to achieve his highest game score for *Ultimate Battle Warrior*. All he wanted was to *be* the new high scorer. He'd been focused on this game all week, and he was almost there . . . almost.

He pounded, pounded, *pounded* on his opponent.

Bam! Took that sucker down!

Winner flashed across the screen.

Toby pushed off the game, raised his arms in victory.

"Heck yeah!"

Someone patted his back. "All right, Toby!"

"Take that, sucker!" Toby punched the air, grinning.

"You *had* to take first place this time, Toby."

Toby expelled a breath, cracked his knuckles, then took a moment to enter his TAB initials, tapping his foot as he waited for the top scores to flash on the screen.

His smile fell away as he blinked in disbelief.

No. Freaking. Way. He still held second place.

Defeat sunk like a rock in his gut.

"Aw, nah, your bro is *still* the highest score. What a drag!"

Toby's hands clenched on the controls. Sure enough, his older brother Connor's initials, COB, were still listed as number one.

Always number one.

Jaw tight, he slammed his palms hard on the game. *Dang it!*

Kids started to walk away except for this annoying guy named Reggie.

"Don't worry about it," Reggie said, slurping a milkshake. His hair was a mass of red curls, flaring out like a halo around his head. "You'll get a game over him, eventually. You're just one thousand points behind. That's practically nothin'."

Toby curled his lip. Every game in Freddy Fazbear's Pizza and Games had his brother listed as the top player. He thought he had this one for sure. He cracked his knuckles and turned away from the stupid game. Then he grabbed his soda cup from a small table next to him and sipped flat root beer through the straw.

"There's still *Hide-and-Seek*," Reggie went on. "It just opened up a week ago, and your brother hasn't even played that one yet. I mean, I haven't seen him, anyway. And you still have to play it. When you do, you'll have the advantage. No problem."

No, he hadn't told his brother a new game attraction had opened at Freddy's just for that exact reason. Toby wanted to play it first and snag the top spot. His brother used to have a part-time job at Freddy's when he was in high school. He'd spent his breaks and after-work hours playing all the arcade games in the place until he'd become the top scorer on every single game. Now that he'd graduated last year and moved on to—in his words—*a real job*, Toby had taken over his old job helping out with cleaning around the family restaurant.

Man, he wanted to beat his brother at a game just once.

Was that too much to ask?

Toby adjusted the beanie on his head. "Yeah, I guess." He'd been watching the long lines die down on the new game, waiting for all the dumb little kids to finish playing. It was a half hour before his shift started, and he had some time to play a round to get a feel for the game.

"Later," he muttered to Reggie.

"Go get 'em, Toby!" the kid yelled, then followed with some annoying howling noise.

That dude was such a weirdo.

Toby heard bowling balls crash into pins from the small bowling alley as he walked through the crowd in the arcade area. Voices and game sounds melded together, echoing in his ears. They were all sounds he'd grown accustomed to in the six months he'd worked at the restaurant. He smelled buttery popcorn, cotton candy, and, of course, pizza, with the occasional stink bomb that came from being close to a bunch of sweaty kids. He walked past laser tag and the prize store, and finally stopped at the door of the new game attraction, *Hide-and-Seek*. A black-shadowed Bonnie the Rabbit stood beside the logo.

Come find me if you can! was printed under the title of the game.

Toby slipped in his tokens, and the game door unlocked. He walked through the doorway, examining the details of the game as an instrumental beat played through the speakers. Inside, the room was sectioned off in parts of a town, with a railing that glided up and down the wall and ended behind board cutouts. There was a park that led to a store, a school, a police station, and, of course, a pizza place. Each section had about three board cutouts that Bonnie could hide behind. There was a thin barricade posted around the walls so kids wouldn't mess with the game. The rules flashed above on a large screen hanging from the ceiling.

THE RULES ARE SIMPLE . . .

FIND WHERE BONNIE IS HIDING IN 3 TRIES IN

UNDER 3 MINUTES

OR LOSE THE GAME!

"Welcome to Hide-and-Seek! *Enter your name to try to find Bonnie, and let's begin!"* a deep voice bellowed out of a wall speaker.

Toby cracked his knuckles. "No problem," he murmured. He typed in his name as the current player. "You're mine, rabbit."

"Here we go, Toby!"

A black two-dimensional cutout of Bonnie glided along

the railing on the wall. The room darkened to pitch-black. Toby heard the quiet sound of Bonnie moving along the railing of the room.

"Three . . . two . . . one!"

The lights flashed back on.

Toby blinked. Bonnie was nowhere to be seen.

He pulled the toothpick from his mouth and rolled it between his fingers. He bit his bottom lip as he assessed the hiding places. He could go anywhere in the game by hitting a button to see where Bonnie might be hiding. He put the toothpick back in his mouth and moved to the police station to hit the button at a desk.

"Sorry, no Bonnie here!"

Toby scanned around the room, rubbing his chin. Had to be the pizza place. He walked over and hit the button for the kitchen doors. *"Sorry, no Bonnie here!"*

One more try . . .

He moved to hit the button for the principal's office at the school.

"Uh-oh, you lose!"

Bonnie glided out of a jail cell at the police station.

"Better luck next time, Toby!"

Toby curled his lip. Not much to the game, but he still wanted to win. He looked up at the screen hanging from the ceiling. Someone already snagged the top score by being the fastest time. Tom at 2:58.

That's nothin'.

Toby turned when he heard the door unlock behind him.

"Welcome to Hide-and-Seek! *Enter your name to try to find Bonnie, and let's begin!"*

A little kid walked in, sporting a Freddy Fazbear party hat. "Hey, it's my turn now," he said, his bottom lip sticking out.

Toby dug out more tokens and slapped them in the kid's hand. He grabbed the kid's shoulder, shoving him back out the door.

"I still got one more turn," he told him.

"Hey, no fair! It's my turn!"

"Stop your whining. I'll be out in a minute." Toby slammed the door on the kid and went to type in his name again.

"Here we go, Toby!"

Bonnie glided out, the room blackened, and the countdown began. He heard Bonnie move quietly. As soon as the lights flashed on, Toby ran to the store and pushed the bakery counter.

"Sorry, no Bonnie here!"

He ran to the park and chose a tree.

"Sorry, no Bonnie here!"

Toby gritted his teeth and ran to the pizza place, pounding his palm on the arcade.

"Uh-oh, you lose!"

Bonnie glided out of the bushes at the park.

"Better luck next time, Toby!"

Toby spit out his toothpick on the floor as annoyance

burned in his gut. He fisted his hands and stormed out the exit door to start his shift.

Stupid game.

Toby walked into his house after work. He heard the television playing, and he rolled his eyes. That meant Connor was home. Great. Dad worked the graveyard shift at a warehouse and wasn't home most nights, so usually it was just him and his brother.

Toby plopped a box of leftover pizza on the kitchen table, then dug out a piece of pepperoni. He was already irritated because he'd played *Hide-and-Seek* a few more times before he came home and he still hadn't found the rabbit. The game wasn't that complicated. How hard could it be to find a hidden rabbit?

"That you, Tobes?" Connor called out.

Who else would it be? Toby walked to the front room and leaned against the wall. "Yeah." Connor was kicked back in Dad's recliner watching baseball. He wore a dirty button-up shirt stained with black grease. Grease was smeared on his cheek and arms. Only his hands were somewhat cleaner, with black oil under his nails.

Connor turned to look at Toby and grinned.

Beat me at any games?

"Beat me at any games yet, little brother?" Connor wanted to know.

Gee, how did he know he'd ask? Toby bit into his pizza and chewed. "Nope."

Connor laughed. "Didn't think so. Not gonna happen. Ever. But it's flattering that you keep trying."

Toby narrowed his eyes. "Oh, it'll happen."

Connor lifted his eyebrows. "Maybe when pigs fly, sucker."

Toby crossed his arms against his chest. He wanted to tell Connor someone else already had the first score on a new game at the pizza place, but he bit his lip. Nah. He wanted to get the lead score first, and he didn't want his brother anywhere near Freddy's until Toby held first place.

Toby pointed at him with his pizza slice. "Pigs will be flying. You'll see, and you'll be the sucker, and I'll be the winner."

"Oh, please."

"Then you won't even know what to do with yourself except go cry in your room."

Connor wasn't deterred; he leaned forward in the recliner. "Oh, you mean like that time you beat my overall home runs during Little League? Or how about all those times you smashed me at bowling?"

Toby scowled. "Just shut up, Connor."

"Oh, I know, you must mean your overall time for the mile run in PE class? You're such a real speedster, aren't you, Tobes?"

Toby pushed off the wall. "I said, SHUT UP!"

Connor's eyes widened. "Oh, wait, you've *never* beaten me in *anything*. And you never will because you're a *pitiful loser* who can't win at anything!"

Toby saw red. He threw his pizza at his brother—Connor smiled in glee as he dodged the slice—and Toby launched himself at Connor in the recliner. He had a moment of satisfaction when his fist hit his brother's gut. Connor grunted.

"Oh, you're going to pay for that," Connor hissed out.

Fists flew. Toby was lifted, tossed on the floor. He hit carpet. Breath rushed out of his mouth. His brother clocked him in the chin, then maneuvered him into a strong arm around his neck.

Toby's face heated. He was losing air. He tapped his brother's arm.

His brother released him and shoved him to the side while Toby coughed.

Shoulders heaving, Connor pointed a finger down at him. "I always beat you at everything, idiot. When are you going to get that through your thick head? I will always win, and you will always lose like the loser you were born to be." Connor left the room, leaving Toby on the floor.

Toby just lay sprawled on the floor, breathing hard, staring at the ceiling.

The next day, Toby studied a block of wood in woodshop class, rubbing his chin with his forefinger. Buzz saws and drills sounded around him. The scent of freshly cut wood filled his nostrils. He was supposed to be working on a small cutting board project, but he had other ideas at the moment—like making rail blocks for *Hide-and-Seek* so that the rabbit couldn't hide in some of the areas in the game.

Yeah, it was cheating.

He just didn't care.

For once, he wanted to shove a winning score right in his brother's face. He felt tension grip his body inch by inch just thinking about Connor. How he always had to be number one at everything he did. How he always had to rub it in Toby's face.

Well, he wasn't going to be a loser this time if it was the last thing he did.

Everything had been a big competition with Connor as far back as Toby could remember. Connor always had to have the best score, the best grades, the biggest piece of cake. He had to be stronger than Toby in arm wrestling, beat him at boxing, and win one-on-one in basketball. He had to get the most attention from Dad, and Mom when she'd been around. He'd been a star quarterback his junior varsity season until he'd banged up his knee and couldn't play well enough afterward. That had really messed with his brother's head. Toby remembered him moping around the house for months. Toby had even felt bad for him for a little while. Until Connor had gotten a job at Freddy's and went on an arcade game mission defeating every high score in the place. He'd been obnoxious and unbearable ever since then. Now that Toby worked there, Connor held that ultimate arcade victory over Toby nearly every day.

It drove Toby freaking crazy.

That was why Connor's reign was finally coming to an end.

Determined, Toby got to work on the block of wood, cutting out squares that would soon be the perfect rail blocks for *Hide-and-Seek*.

Mr. Pedrick walked by Toby's workstation. He adjusted his glasses and looked at Toby cutting out blocks. "Those are too small for a cutting board, Toby."

"Yeah, I know. I'm getting to the cutting board next."

Mr. Pedrick crossed his arms. "The cutting board is your assignment now. It's due at the end of the period. How are you going to get it done in thirty minutes? You're a good kid, Toby. I know you can do better than this if you just try and put some effort into your projects."

"I'm starting the project right now." Irritated, Toby walked over to the wood table and picked up another piece of wood for the cutting board. When Mr. Pedrick walked away, he set the new piece of wood aside and continued with the rail blocks. Some things were more important and took priority over schoolwork.

Like beating an annoying, ignorant, loudmouthed brother.

After Freddy Fazbear's Pizza and Games closed that night, Toby inserted his coins for a new round of *Hide-and-Seek*. There were only a couple of employees left cleaning up in the kitchen and he'd snuck inside the game room near the end of his shift. The game voice welcomed him to the game. Before Toby entered his name, he walked over to the small barricaded fence that blocked the wall from players getting too close to the game and hopped over. From his sweatshirt, he dug out the small wooden blocks that he'd shaped to fit in the railing. He gave the blocks a good pound with his hand, wedging each wood piece into the rails to cut off access to the school, police station, and the pizza place. Now the only places the rabbit could hide were the park and the store, which were right next to each other.

Toby smiled and nodded. Now he would definitely win, and he'd get his name listed as first place.

Oh yeah, let's do this!

He couldn't wait to rub Connor's face in his win. He could see his brother now: His face would get all red, just like it did whenever something didn't go his way, and he'd storm off and hit a wall in the house like a big baby. Dad would yell at him to go cool off, and then Dad would look at Toby and roll his eyes.

Toby snickered. It would be priceless.

Toby hopped back over the small fence and ran to enter his name into the game.

"Here we go, Toby!"

"Yeah, here we go, rabbit."

Bonnie glided out, the room blackened.

"Three . . ."

Toby tapped his foot as he waited for the lights to turn on.

"*Two . . . one!*"

As soon as the room brightened, he sprinted to the park and slapped on the slide.

"*Sorry, no Bonnie here!*"

He hit the tree.

"*Sorry, no Bonnie here!*"

Rattled, he hit the deli at the store.

"*Uh-oh, you lose!*"

Toby's jaw dropped in disbelief! His peppermint-flavored toothpick fell to the floor. *No freaking way!*

Bonnie glided from behind the cashier register at the store.

"*Better luck next time, Toby!*"

Toby's hands fisted as he growled loudly in frustration. "You think you're funny, don't you, rabbit? You think I'm a loser? Well, I'm not, you idiot! You're the loser! You'll see!"

He paced back and forth, and tore the beanie from his head. His entire body vibrated with tension. "I am not going to lose another game to you!" He rubbed his hands over his head. "Think. *Think!*"

He wanted to win. He *needed* to win.

Suddenly, he whirled as a quick solution crossed his mind. "Yes!" He rushed out of the game room. A minute later, he inserted his tokens and came back in, carrying two metal chairs. He already had the store, the school, and pizza place covered. He wedged the back of the chairs into the railing to the park and the store. The bottom of the chairs leaned forward on the small fence.

"Welcome to Hide-and-Seek! Enter your name to try to find Bonnie, and let's begin!"

"Yeah, yeah," he muttered. Toby stood back, hands on his hips, looking at his handiwork. Everywhere was blocked. There was no way the rabbit could even hide at all!

"Hah! Got you now, sucker. Who's the winner now?"

He rubbed his damp palms together as he rushed to input his name. He felt a sheen of sweat on his forehead and wiped it with the back of his hand. He felt jittery. Off. Like he couldn't keep still. He rolled his neck in a circular motion and cracked his knuckles.

"Here we go, Toby!" the voice sang out.

Bonnie glided out, the room blackened.

"Three . . ."

Toby's stomach took a sudden dive and his head went light. He almost felt like puking.

"Two . . ."

For one moment, a rush of quiet seemed to fill the room. As if all the air was sucked out of the area and his ears were about to pop. He felt a strange tickle at his back and shifted a shoulder to make it go away. Then all at once, sound rushed back into his ears.

"One!"

The lights flashed on.

Toby blinked. He felt disoriented. He rubbed his eyes and scanned the walls before him. "Wait." Bonnie . . . was gone.

Toby's head swiveled left and right. Even to the ceiling.

There was no way the rabbit should be able to hide any-where. "What the heck? Where'd you go?"

He rushed to the small fenced barricade and hopped over to the billboard cutouts, trying to peer inside the slight gap between the cutouts and the wall.

The slots were empty.

No, this wasn't right. His stomach was turning and his chest felt tight. He continued to run to each cutout, peer-ing behind the wooden displays. There was nowhere the rabbit could have gone. This didn't make any sense. Toby's heart beat like a drum. A bead of sweat dripped down the side of his head.

No, no, no.

This wasn't fair! The stupid rabbit couldn't win!

Heat flashed across his face. A burst of helpless energy flared throughout his body. His breaths increased. He wasn't a loser.

He wasn't a freaking loser!

He ran to the chair he'd propped against the railing, picked it up, and heaved it across the room. It smashed against a wall, denting a hole into the game's pizza place. He pulled at one part of the small fence and tore it down. He stomped through the broken barrier and stalked over to the other chair and threw it against another wall. He pulled down another section of the fencing, reached for the tree cutout at the park, and gritting his teeth, he pulled at it with all his strength. It ripped off the wall as he crashed to the floor. Only a few pegs stuck out in its place. He threw the tree, got back to his feet, and ran to the police station, tearing at the desk cutout.

I always beat you at everything, idiot. When are you going to get that through your thick head? I will always win, and you will always lose like the loser you were born to be.

He tugged and tore at anything he could get his hands on. He wasn't sure how long he went at it. Tearing down. Destroying. All he knew was that he had to be rid of this helpless feeling within him. This feeling of being weak and powerless. This pain that always seemed to be inside of him. He hated it.

He needed it out! Gone!

Finally, his body grew tired as he tripped on a piece of a cutout and fell on his ass. His chest was heaving up and down. Sweat covered his face. His hands were red and throbbing. He looked around at what he'd done and satisfaction filled him.

Yeah, take that, he thought.

He'd pretty much destroyed *Hide-and-Seek.*

As he stared at the destruction, reality crashed down on him. He swallowed past the dryness in his throat. He scrubbed at his face with his hands, then continued to stare at the mess he'd created. He'd ruined a game that wasn't his. He was going to get in so much trouble.

Frantic, he stood and grabbed the tree he'd torn from the wall. He quickly tried to reattach it to the pegs, but it was no use. It just crashed back to the floor.

"What did I do?" he whispered. Then he did the only thing he could think to do: he ran out of the room.

Toby opened his eyes. Blinked. He was in the dark. He was lying facedown on a cold metal table. Where was he? Bright lights flashed on above him and he squinted. He tried to sit up but his hands were tied above his head. His legs were bound at his ankles, and he couldn't move them.

"What the heck?" Toby tried to lift his head a little. "Hey! What's going on? Connor? Are you messing with me?" His voice seemed to echo inside the room. He looked around to see brick walls surrounding him. "You're going to get busted for doing this."

Someone shifted behind him.

When no one answered, panic set in. Connor would have been blabbing his mouth by now. "Hey, whoever you are, you better let me go!" He jerked at his hands, but the rope just bit into his wrists, rubbing his skin raw. His heartbeats seemed to pound against the cold table beneath him. Then he spotted something dark in his peripheral vision.

"What do you want?" He felt his shirt tugged from his back, then heard scissors cutting at it. "Stop it! Leave me alone!" Cold air hit his skin. He heard more movement, then something small bit into his back. Like a needle. "Ow! Don't touch me!"

The needle was pulled out, and then he felt his skin being tugged. "What the heck are you doing to me?" He jerked his head left and right, trying to see what was happening. Sweat pearled on his forehead. Again, he felt the needle push into his skin and then pull. Blood dripped down his back as the pain grew in intensity.

"Stop, you're hurting me! Please, I said, stop!"

But whoever the dark figure was, he didn't speak.

And he didn't stop.

Toby felt every prick and pull of the needle as realization dawned.

Someone was sewing something to his back.

"Someone help me!" he screamed. "Please!"

Toby jerked awake. He sat up in his bed, alert. Heart pounding. Breathing fast. He was disoriented. It was just a bad dream. Sunlight slanted through his window blinds. He was okay. He was home. What day was it? Was it time to go to school? Did he oversleep? He glanced at his alarm clock: 7:55 a.m. He didn't set his alarm because it was Saturday. Right?

He rubbed his face, then glanced at the mirror mounted on his dresser across from his bed. His face was pale, and there were dark circles under his eyes. His brown hair stuck up in crazy directions. He spotted his shadow on the wall behind him and felt a ticklish feeling at his back.

A shadow?

Frowning, he tilted his head as he looked at it in the reflection of the mirror. That didn't seem right. There wasn't enough light from the window blinds for him to see his own shadow in his room. He shifted and leaned to the right. A second later, the shadow followed.

Toby's eyes widened. Did his own shadow just delay in following him?

He leaned quickly to the left. But this time, the shadow moved quickly.

He shook his head. *Weird.* He probably wasn't fully awake yet.

Toby yawned and scratched his chest, then stretched his arms over his head. The shadow followed along. Then he winced. His body was sore. Guilt from last night came crashing back. Dang, why did he have to mess up the game like that? What was Dan, his boss, going to say? Was he going to get caught? When he put his arms down, the shadow's arms were still up.

Toby sucked in a breath and jumped from his bed. Looking at the wall behind his bed, he saw nothing. No shadow. He whipped his head toward the mirror and saw the shadow behind him.

A chill radiated down his spine.

He stepped closer to the large mirror on his dresser, watching as the shadow followed closely behind. The closer he got, the dark shadow followed. He peered into the mirror, and his mouth went dry.

The shadow had . . . rabbit ears.

Toby spun around as if he could somehow catch the shadow. But every time he turned, there was nothing behind him. It was as if it would suddenly duck and hide somewhere in his room. Toby went to his bed and peered underneath. Just a bunch of dust and junk. He went to his closet and saw more junk. But even that didn't make sense. He glanced back in the mirror, and the shadow was still behind him.

The only rabbit he could even think of was Bonnie the Rabbit from the game *Hide-and-Seek*.

Toby froze for a moment, trying to comprehend what was actually happening. A rabbit's shadow from a game attached to his back. He frowned. Wait, this couldn't be real. Suddenly, relief seeped through him. He slapped a hand to his forehead and barked out a laugh.

"I'm still dreaming. *Duh*." There was *no way* he could actually be seeing a shadow in the shape of a rabbit. This was some nightmare he was having because he was afraid he'd get caught for breaking the dumb game. Everything was fine, he assured himself. He yawned again and decided to go back to bed. When he would really wake up again, the only shadow he'd see would be his own. He climbed back into bed and got underneath the covers. He looked once more into the mirror, seeing the shadow hovering behind him.

Toby waved, and the shadow waved with him.

He lay down and closed his eyes, drifting off to sleep.

Toby blinked awake. His eyes were blurry. He rubbed his eyes and yawned, stretching his sore body. Even though he'd slept in, he felt exhausted. He sat up in bed, glancing into the dresser mirror.

The shadow was still there.

Fear punched his chest, and he pushed back against the

wall, kicking the covers off of him. He sprang out of bed, hunched down, staring at the mirror. The shadow lurked just at his back. Toby reached behind him as if he could feel the shadow, but he only grabbed air.

He swallowed hard as he stood straight, and the shadow did the same. He turned to his side to see if he could see the shadow closely, but for some reason, the shadow stayed just behind him.

"Who are you?" he asked the shadow. "What do you want?"

The shadow didn't speak.

"Get away from me."

Nothing happened.

"I said, GO AWAY!"

Nothing.

Toby gritted his teeth as he paced back and forth, rubbing his hands hard through his hair. Okay, there was a shadow following him that wasn't his own shadow. How could this be happening? This was too freaking weird. He stopped again, leaning onto the dresser with his hands, and peered into the mirror. Every time he saw the darkness behind him, a chill ran through his entire body, making him shiver. Did his back feel heavier than usual? Toby was pretty sure it was because that thing was attached to him. What should he do? Well, he knew what he should do. He needed to get it off of him. But how could he make it go away?

"I can do this," he murmured. "I can get it off of me. There has to be a way. *Think*."

He bit his bottom lip and glanced at his wall in the reflection of the mirror, staring at it for a moment. He pushed away from the dresser and rubbed his chin as he studied the wall. Abruptly, he turned his back to the wall, sucked in a breath, then blew it out. Then he sucked in another breath and exhaled again. Squeezing his eyes shut, he ran backward and slammed against the bare wall. He'd knocked the wind from his mouth. His entire body vibrated. He lunged forward and then slammed back— *hard*—against the wall again, and again. Pain radiated down his spine as he fell to the floor, wincing.

A sheen of sweat sprang across his forehead as he crawled to his dresser, his back throbbing. He reached up and pulled himself to his feet, staring into the mirror.

The shadow still lurked behind him.

He threw himself helplessly onto his bed and screamed into his pillow.

Nervous and bruised, Toby dressed, avoiding the mirror. He left his room and went to the kitchen. The feeling that someone was at his back wouldn't go away. It was like he was being watched.

He felt stalked. *Trapped.*

There was a pile of dishes in the sink and the scent of burnt bacon and eggs. Whose turn was it to do the dishes? Probably his, but he didn't care. Toby turned and stepped into the front room. His dad was in shorts and a T-shirt, kicked back in his recliner, blurry-eyed, and drinking coffee.

Toby swallowed hard and cracked his knuckles. "Hey, Dad."

Dad grunted and looked over at Toby. "Mornin', Tobes."

"Morning." Toby's hands were shaking. He fisted them into a tight grip. "Um, Dad, you see anything different about me?"

His dad squinted at him, looking him up and down. "Look the same to me. You do something different?" He scratched at the scruff on his chin as he studied him. "You finally growing some hair above your lip?"

Toby shook his head right away. "No. Just askin' if you could see anything out of the ordinary. Something . . . that's not supposed to be there."

Just then, Connor strolled in. "Don't worry, Tobes. You're still the same little loser. Nothing's changed."

"Shut up, Connor," he said, but without his usual heat.

Connor reached out and rubbed Toby's head. Toby shoved him away.

"Neither of you . . . see my shadow?" Toby asked them. "Really?"

Connor made a face. "What are you talking about, idiot?"

He stretched his arms out. "A shadow, *idiot*. Do you see it or what? Can't you answer a simple question?"

Connor looked around Toby, shaking his head as he walked to the kitchen. "You got problems, Tobes."

Toby rounded on his dad, who just ignored him and continued to watch sports.

How could they not see that there was a weird darkness following him around?

Was he still dreaming? No, he was definitely wide awake. His back was still hurting from slamming against the wall. Was he the only one who could see it? Did that make him crazy? Had Connor finally driven him nuts?

He went to his dad, leaned toward him. "Dad, feel my head." Dad smelled of coffee and cigarettes. His eyes were a little bloodshot.

Dad sighed. "Tobes, what's the matter with ya?" He put his hand on his forehead. "No, you're good, son. So don't get any ideas about skipping school, all right? Then I start getting a bunch of calls and texts from the school while I'm trying to sleep before my shift."

Toby straightened. "I'm not."

The phone rang. Connor answered. "Yeah? Yep, hold on. Hey, idiot, it's for you. Work."

Toby's gut flipped. *Oh no, no, no.* He walked over to Connor as he snickered at him. Toby snatched the phone away from him. "Yeah. Hello?"

"Toby, it's Dan. Can you come to work? I need to talk to you about something. Very important."

Toby scratched his neck. "Um, yeah, sure."

"All right. See you soon."

"Okay." Toby hung up.

Connor widened his eyes. "Ooooh, Tobes is in trouble. What'd you do now?"

Toby schooled his expression to innocence, which was kind of hard. "Nothing."

Connor shook his head. "Dan never calls employees unless they mess up royally. What'd you do? Forget to lock up something? Or you broke something and didn't tell him?"

Toby narrowed his eyes at his brother. Did he know something? "I didn't mess up. He's probably calling me in to tell me what a fantastic job I've been doing. So much better than you ever did."

"Yeah, right. I do everything better than you. Even that stupid job."

"Holy cow!" Dad yelled from the front room. "Bases loaded, baby! Boys, get in here! This game is getting good!"

Connor lost interest in Toby and strode into the front room, joining Dad. "What I tell ya? They got this game easy! I always pick the winning team, right, Dad?"

Dad laughed. "You do, son, you do!"

Toby rolled his eyes and walked back to his room. He realized he wasn't hungry at all. He really couldn't argue with his brother about him doing a better job at Freddy's at the moment. He'd messed up royally by breaking *Hide-and-Seek*. He didn't know what was going to happen when he talked to Dan. He looked into the mirror, and the shadow lurked behind him like a dark ghost that wouldn't leave him alone. He shuddered. He looked at his hands. Still shaking. This whole thing was freaking him out. Toby slapped a beanie on his head and took a breath in an attempt to calm his nerves. He had to face Dan about *Hide-and-Seek*. Then he'd figure out what to do about the shadow.

Dan lifted his beefy arm to encompass the entire disaster area of *Hide-and-Seek*. "Can you believe it? I just opened this game, and now it's destroyed." Dan was built like a bull. All big-chested with meaty arms, but with short, skinny legs. He was an okay boss and was always cool to Toby. That was why Toby felt pretty bad for messing up his game.

Toby stared at the chaos of the room with wide eyes. The game looked even worse than he remembered. The screen was dead now. Dan must have shut it down. Nearly all the cutouts were torn from the wall. Only pegs were left sticking out as placeholders. Most of the cutouts were broken. Some split totally in half. There were a few dents in the walls.

"I—I can't believe it," Toby said, cracking his knuckles. He couldn't believe he'd done all this damage by himself.

Dan turned to Toby, eyeing him with intensity. "Do you have any idea who did this?"

Toby shook his head as guilt weighed heavy on his conscience. "No, Dan. I don't know who could have done this."

"You didn't see anyone suspicious messing around last night? You checked the bathroom stalls, right? The play area? No one was hiding anywhere after closing?"

"Yeah, I did the routine check like you always tell me. No, I didn't see anyone suspicious."

Dan ran a hand down his thick beard. "Really ticks me off, you know? I put good money into this place for people to enjoy, and this is how I'm repaid? Ticks me off."

"Yeah, I bet."

"When I was a kid, they didn't have places like these. Kids played outdoors and just went and had a pizza. But I liked the idea of families coming together to eat and play together, have a party. This place isn't much, but it's a dream of mine, so it really upsets me when something like this happens." Dan sighed. "Well, I got to get the technician in here and see what he can do. Thanks for coming in, Toby."

Toby nodded. "Let me help you clean up."

Dan placed his hands on his hips. "Sure, but I got to keep all the parts for insurance. The police already took pictures."

Toby felt a clinch in his gut. "The police?"

"Yeah, I had to report this as a break-in and vandalism. They may need to ask you some questions. They're talking to everyone who worked last night."

Toby swallowed hard and nodded. "Sure. No problem."

"If you could pick up the big pieces and set them in a pile and sweep up the small stuff, that would be helpful."

"Sure."

"Thanks, Toby. You're a good kid." Dan stomped out of the game room, muttering something under his breath.

Toby's shoulders slumped as he started to clean up the floor. He piled the big cutouts against one wall. When he picked up the cutout of the bushes, he saw his beanie from last night. His heart skipped a beat as he looked behind him to see if anyone had come into the room. He quickly swiped it up and stuck it into his back pocket. Suddenly, his head jerked to the railing. The wooden blocks he'd made were still jammed inside. He picked up a long piece of broken wood and started to pry them out of the rail, one by one. Heart pounding, he hurriedly picked up the three pieces from the floor, and stashed them in his sweatshirt. Then, taking a breath, he continued to clean up his mess.

Toby felt awful the rest of the weekend. He mostly stayed in his room. He put an old sheet over his mirror. Even though he knew the shadow was still there, he didn't want to have to look at it. Every time he did, his pulse fluttered, and he started to shake because it wasn't supposed to be there. It was like this scary, dark, hidden secret.

He ate almost nothing on Sunday and barely slept. He didn't talk to his dad or his brother. Dad knocked on his door to check on him, but he told him he was just tired. He heard them yelling at some game on the television. Dad, Connor, and Toby were pretty close, but Dad and Connor had this obsession with sports that they'd always shared. Dad was either working a lot or sleeping, but when he wasn't, he was hanging out with Connor, watching sports and having a good old time. Since Toby wasn't that into sports, that didn't leave much for Dad-and-Toby time.

Toby guessed he'd been closer to his mom, but he wasn't sure since she left one day when Toby was about five and Connor seven. He had a vague memory of Dad bringing them home from Connor's Little League practice and Mom just being gone. Dad had called for her, and then Connor ran around the house looking for her. Dad had found a letter on the kitchen table. Connor asked what it said and wanted to know where Mom was, but Dad just read the letter, then crumbled it in his hand and walked away. That night was the first of hundreds of frozen dinners together. No explanation to Toby and Connor was given about Mom, so they just continued on with life as if Mom had never been around. Maybe that was when Connor really started attempting to be the best at everything. Toby wasn't sure. His brother could have just been born with a screw loose.

Toby skipped school on Monday, but he did decide to go to his shift at Freddy's that afternoon. He didn't know if he could pull the shift off. His energy was spent, his back felt tight and heavy, and all he wanted to do was lie down and go to sleep.

He walked into Freddy's, and Reggie met him in the arcade. He had a slice of pizza in his hand. "Dude, you look gnarly." He chomped on his pizza.

Toby just shrugged as he walked past him.

"Whoa, what's with the shadow? Looks intense."

Toby's eyes widened as he whirled. He rushed to Reggie and grabbed the front of his shirt with both hands. *"You can see it?"*

"Take it easy. Uh, yeah. Your shadow is way dark, dude." He bit into his slice and chewed in front of Toby's face.

"I can't get rid of it. It's freaking me out."

Reggie lifted his eyebrows. "I bet. How'd you get it, anyway?"

Toby let him go and jerked a shoulder. "Dunno. Just happened. A freak thing."

"I get it, man, it's personal." Reggie smoothed his shirt with his other hand. "That really sucks you got to deal with it."

"Yeah. But you're the only one who's said they've seen it."

Reggie nodded, and his red curls moved with the motion. "Totally see it."

"Do you see the ears?"

Reggie frowned. "Huh?"

Toby shook his head. "Never mind. *How* can you even see it?"

Reggie shrugged. "People say I see things differently."

Toby stared at him when he didn't elaborate. "Whatever. I think it's . . ."

Reggie took another bite of pizza. "What?"

"I think it's from a game I . . . uh . . . cheated."

"Oh yeah? Which game?"

Toby wasn't sure he could truly trust him. He was a regular at Freddy's, and he could tell Dan whatever he told him. "Doesn't matter. I just need to get rid of it. I can't keep walking around with this thing at my back. It's weird."

"Well, if I were you, I'd try anything to get that thing off of me like yesterday." Reggie shuddered. "Looks totally creepy, dude."

Just seeing Reggie's reaction made him shudder in return. "Like try what? I don't know how to make it go away. What do you think I should do?"

"Dude, you're a gamer. Use your imagination. I've watched you for weeks attempt to beat your brother's score on nearly every game in this arcade. That takes fire, you know? Where's that fire now?"

Toby stiffened, cracked his knuckles. "I got fire."

Reggie nodded. "Then get to it, bro."

That night, Toby thought about what Reggie said, and he felt inspired. He wasn't defeated yet. He could beat the shadow and get it off of him. He could freaking win this game. He made a list.

IDEAS TO REMOVE SHADOW:

SLAM IT OFF (DIDN'T WORK)

SCRUB IT OFF

DROWN IT OFF

BURN IT OFF (FORGET THAT)

CUT IT OFF (MAYBE)

Toby went into the garage. He searched around the clutter for the car-wash scrubber on a stick. No one had washed their cars in forever, but Toby knew the scrubber was still around somewhere. It had thick bristles that just might scrub the shadow right off his back.

It could totally work.

Maybe.

He was pretty much willing to try anything to get this thing off of him.

He kicked at boxes, making a path around the garage. Shoved the lawn mower and kicked a deflated football. *Holy heck!* He jumped when a little mouse skittered across the floor. He needed to remember to tell his dad to buy some mousetraps. He finally found the scrubber stuck in a corner with an old wash bucket. He grabbed the scrubber and tried to reach it over his back, but the stick was too long.

He looked around and found a rusted saw in his dad's old toolbox. He leaned the stick on the washer with his left hand, and started sawing away at the stick with his right. The blade was dull and it took a few minutes, but a part of the stick finally broke off, dropping to the floor.

Toby lifted the scrubber in his hand and felt the bristles with his fingers. "Yeah, nice and thick. You'll do."

He tipped the brush onto his back and gave a rub. It would definitely work. Determined, he took off his shirt and laid it on the dryer. Then he took a breath, grabbed the stick with both hands, and started scrubbing his back. *Hard.*

"Ow, ow, ow." He scrubbed, wincing. The bristles bit into his skin. Scraping. Scratching. "See how you like that," he muttered. He scrubbed and he scrubbed at his back, feeling the skin peel away to rawness. "Jeez, this hurts." He scrubbed till he felt like his back was burning, and he couldn't take it anymore. Trembling, he dropped the scrubber and fell to his knees, sucking air through his teeth. His vision dimmed, and he blinked.

"Please let this work. Please," he whispered.

Exhausted and in pain, he grabbed his shirt and carefully slid it over his head. Then he got to his feet and stumbled back into the house and to his room.

Toby leaned against his dresser and slowly pulled off the sheet covering the mirror. He looked awful. His eyes were wild. His brown hair was stuck on his forehead with sweat. His face was pale, and his skin looked dry.

He lifted his gaze to look behind him. The shadow loomed at his back, and it seemed to be bigger, even darker. It moved as Toby's shoulders heaved.

"No," he said. It hadn't worked.

He may not have gotten the shadow off his back, but he apparently ticked it off. He could feel its anger, its darkness, more intensely. Feeling the emotions was like being squeezed into too small a box, and the sides were closing in, suffocating him.

Toby pounded a fist on his dresser. "I hate you," he said. "I hate you!" Then he felt himself falling, and everything went black.

★ ★ ★

Toby jerked awake and hit his knee on something hard. "Ow." Saliva drooled from his mouth, and he wiped it away with the back of his hand. He heard knocking. He lifted his head and looked around. Clothes were littered around him. He was on the floor of his bedroom at the foot of his bed. He'd hit his knee on his dresser. He'd slept on the floor all night?

More knocking on his door. "Toby, get up! Dad said you have to go to school today!" Connor bellowed through the door.

"All right, I'm up!" he yelled, and settled his head back on the carpet.

He heard his brother walk away. Toby slowly sat up, wincing. His head felt like it wanted to fall off. His back burned as if on fire. He pushed himself to his feet, and the room spun. "Oh, dang." He grabbed on to the dresser to keep from falling again and waited for the room to stop spinning.

Even though he wasn't hungry, he had to eat something to keep up his energy. He didn't care to look in the mirror. He knew the shadow was still there. He could feel its weight, could sense the darkness looming over him like a threat.

Toby managed to shower first without falling over, but the spray hurt too badly, so he didn't let the water run down his back. He brushed his teeth, ignoring the shadow as it followed along in the bathroom mirror. He dressed and walked into the kitchen. His brother sat at the table, eating cereal, waffles, and two bananas.

Connor stopped mid-chew when he spotted Toby. "You're really sick?"

Toby didn't care to answer.

"You look bad. What's the matter with you?"

Toby just shook his head as he got out cereal and milk, then a bowl and spoon.

"Why aren't you talking, Tobes?"

He shrugged.

"Maybe you should stay home another day."

Toby looked at his brother in surprise. Where were all the stupid remarks? All the put-downs? "I'm going."

When Toby finally answered, Connor seemed satisfied. "All right, but if you got the flu, keep your distance." He wolfed down his cereal, waffles, and both bananas. He threw his dishes in the sink, gave a gnarly burp, and said, "Later." Then he walked out of the kitchen. A moment later, the front door slammed shut.

Toby ate a few spoonfuls of cereal, but after a few minutes, he felt it coming right back up. He ran to the garbage and puked. His body shuddered with spasms.

He managed to straighten, with a hand to his stomach. If he didn't know better, the shadow seemed to be sucking the life out of him. The idea of something overpowering him annoyed the heck out of him.

He clenched his fists. "You are *not* going to win."

★ ★ ★

Toby felt like a zombie at school. He walked the halls slow and tired. Kids stared at him as he passed, then looked away. Toby stared back, not caring about anything. Teachers didn't care what he did, anyway. He'd never been a star student. In fact, he just went through the motions of school. Dad never cared about his grades. He just wanted him to pass and graduate, so that's what Toby set out to do. He went to school, did the homework he could, skipped the assignments that didn't make any sense, and he got passing grades. Sometimes barely passing, but credits were credits.

When Toby came in as a freshman and teachers discovered he was Connor Billings's little brother, they'd smiled big and asked him questions. Connor was so confident, so conversational. Great at sports. He did his best at schoolwork and extracurriculars. A real go-getter. Little brother Toby had to be the same—it ran in the family, right?

Wrong. They found out quickly Toby wasn't very outgoing. He never really made friends or joined any clubs. He didn't care to try his best like Connor had. Toby did what he had to do to walk the line up to his senior year. Soon the teachers had stopped being friendly and started getting annoyed. He'd get looks of disapproval, and most of all, he got the looks of disinterest and dismissal . . . like he didn't matter to them.

Well, news flash. The feeling was mutual.

Toby detoured to the restroom before he ambled to his locker. There was a kid with headphones on, messing with his hair in the mirror. He was bopping up and down. Toby used the restroom, and when he turned around to wash his hands, the kid froze, staring into the mirror. His mouth hung open in shock. The kid pointed to Toby, or more likely to the shadow behind him.

Dang it. He must be able to see the shadow in the mirror, too.

Toby cracked his knuckles. "Hey, look . . ."

The kid spun around to look at Toby, frowned, then looked back in the mirror.

Before Toby could say more, the kid booked it out of the bathroom as if he was running from a fire. Or more like a monster from a horror movie.

"Okay, later," Toby muttered as he washed his hands.

Toby had gym class for first period, which he realized was perfect for the next step in his plan. Today his class was scheduled to play basketball.

Mr. Dillonhall, a tall, bald man in a bright tracksuit, blew his whistle. He cocked his hip and leaned his clipboard against his big stomach. "All right! Line up for roll call!"

Toby, dressed in shorts and a T-shirt, lined up with the other kids. He'd been careful to stay away from any mirrors in the locker room. He just hoped he didn't see that scared kid again. That was all he needed, for a weird rumor to start going around school.

A girl walked up and handed Mr. Dillonhall a note.

"What now?" Mr. Dillonhall muttered, then skimmed the note. "Fine, go have a seat." He rolled his eyes dramatically before getting to roll call.

"Billings!" Toby raised his hand when Dillonhall looked up from his chart. "For goodness' sake, let's put some effort in today, Billings. Come on, kid."

Toby just crossed his arms as Mr. Dillonhall continued taking attendance, occasionally making snide remarks to the other kids.

"Dillonhall's such a jerk," murmured Tabitha Bing. Kids called her Tab for short. Toby glanced at her, then turned away. She was sort of an outcast and liked to rebel against the system. She had a nose piercing and wore a lot of black. Occasionally, she started petitions to get things changed around the school. She'd attempted to run for student body president a couple of times, but she'd lost to popular kids. She was always blowing little things out of proportion, in Toby's opinion. Since she seemed to be the total opposite of Toby, he usually steered clear of her.

"You don't talk much, do you, Billings?" she asked him.

Toby turned to her, and this time shrugged. "Don't got much to say at school."

She lifted her eyebrows and smiled. "Unlike me, you mean."

"You said it, not me."

"All right," Dillonhall barked out. "Let's break into your groups and play some basketball. I want to see some serious effort on the court. None of those 'oh, my chest hurts' or 'I twisted my ankle' excuses, people. I want real athletes on the court. Let's go!"

As the groups gathered and started their games, Toby checked out of his group to use the restroom. He left the gym, glancing over his shoulder. No one was around in the hallway. He detoured to the high school pool, which luckily was free for the period. The strong scent of chlorine filled his nostrils as he scanned the clear water.

He couldn't pound the shadow off of him. Nor could he scrub it off. Now it was time for more intense measures.

"Hope you can swim," he said out loud to the shadow. *"Or not."* He looked around for something heavy but couldn't find anything in the pool area to weigh him down. He jogged to the weight room. There were some kids in there, lifting weights, but Toby managed to sneak in and grab a heavy weight vest. Back at the pool, he slipped it onto his shoulders and buckled it at his chest. He bounced on the balls of his feet and felt the vest was a good weight to sink him to the bottom and keep him there. He walked back to the pool and stared at the still water.

He bit his bottom lip. Not that he'd admit it to anyone, but he was a little scared. He could swim, but he wasn't used to holding his breath for a long time. He paced back and forth along the deep end of the pool.

Come on, you can do this.

What could go wrong?

Nothing really.

And hey, this could really work. You could be free of the shadow and get on with your life.

He finally stopped pacing and stood in front of the pool. After taking a big breath, he pinched his nose, and jumped into the deep end.

Toby slowly sank to the bottom of the pool. Even though the school claimed it was heated, the water still felt ice cold. With the vest holding him down, he sat at the bottom and waited. He blinked, looking around the pool area. He could feel the chlorine sting his eyes. He wondered how long he could hold his breath, and he wondered if the shadow could hold his breath at all.

Did shadows even breathe?

He guessed he'd find out.

This has to work, he thought. He couldn't live forever with the darkness at his back. Not only would it drive him crazy, but it would be a constant reminder that he was a failure. A loser.

I will always win and you will always lose like the loser you were born to be.

No, he couldn't live like this forever.

Too fast, it felt like his lungs were squeezing closed, so he pulled at the buckle to release the vest. This was all the time he could manage holding his breath. Hopefully, it was enough to drown the shadow off of him.

But when Toby pinched the release, the buckle wouldn't unlatch. He tried to press the buckle to detach it again, but it wouldn't let go.

A surge of anxiety shot through him. Toby jerked at the buckle, trying to pull it apart. He had the urge to open his mouth to breathe.

Panic clawed at him as adrenaline flooded his system. He pushed himself from the floor with his feet, but the weight of the vest pulled him back down. He pushed up again, paddling his arms, kicking his legs, trying to swim to the top.

But he was too weak from not eating much the last couple of days.

He sank back to the bottom, clawing at the vest.

Oh no. Someone help me! Help!

There was a splash in the pool above him. Someone swam toward him.

Toby couldn't fight it anymore. He opened his mouth and swallowed water as the person pulled him by his vest to the top. Toby kicked with his legs to help get the two of them to the top.

He broke through the surface, gagging up water. Water and snot dripped from his nostrils. The person helped hook his arm onto the edge of the pool. He coughed and sucked in much-needed air. His lungs burned, his entire body shuddering with each breath.

Toby opened his eyes to see a drenched Tabitha Bing in the pool beside him. She was hanging on the side of the pool with one arm. His eyes stung, and he pressed his fingers into them.

"What the heck were you doing?" she snapped at him.

Toby pushed hair out of his eyes, breathing hard. "You . . . wouldn't believe me . . . if I told you."

"Well, it better be a good enough reason for me not to report you to the principal, jerkwad." She pulled herself over the top of the ledge. Water streamed from her soaked PE clothes. Toby tried to climb out as Tabitha pulled his vest, struggling to get him onto the platform. His body felt like dead weight between his drenched clothes and vest.

With both of them helping, they managed to extract Toby from the pool. Toby rolled to his back, and Tabitha fell to the platform beside him.

"For a skinny guy, you weigh a ton." She got to her feet and looked down at him. Water drops streamed down her arms and legs. "Meet me at the soccer field at lunch or I'm going straight to the office to report you."

Toby coughed. "It's not really your business."

"I just saved your life. I'm making it my business. So which is it? Are you meeting me or am I going straight to the office?"

Toby lifted a hand and let it drop. "Yeah, fine. I'll be there."

"I wasn't trying to hurt myself," Toby said grudgingly to Tabitha. They sat together on the soccer field bleachers during lunch break. It was a nice day, but a breeze kept pushing clouds over the sun every so often, making it a little cold. Toby was still chilled from the pool experience, so he huddled inside his sweatshirt. Tabitha's hair was black and pulled away from her freckled face. Normally, she wore makeup, but the pool water must have washed it all off. She was eating a sandwich that smelled like peanut butter.

"Then why the weighted vest?"

"I was just trying to stay down for as long as I could. But the buckle got stuck and I couldn't release it or swim up fast enough." Toby cracked his knuckles. "So, uh, thanks for helping me out."

"Oh, you mean, the saving your life thing?" She waved a hand. "All in a day's work."

"You're a pretty strong swimmer."

"My parents always said I was born to swim. I've been going to junior lifeguard camp forever." She shrugged. "Why did you want to stay down at the bottom of the pool for so long, anyway?"

Toby shook his head. How could he tell her he was trying to drown a shadow attached to his back and that it hadn't worked? When he went in the locker room to change, he saw in the mirror that it was still there behind him. More intense and scarier than before.

"Here, have some of my lunch. You look like you need it," she said, handing him half of her sandwich.

He put a hand to his gut. "Nah, my stomach is upset."

"It's just some bread and peanut butter. Try it."

Toby accepted the half sandwich and took a small bite. It was gooey in his mouth, but he was able to get it down. It seemed he could keep it down as well, he realized with relief.

"Why did you follow me?" Toby asked her.

She ducked her head and shrugged. "You looked . . . I don't know. Like you could use a friend."

Toby didn't have anything to say to that. What does *needing a friend* look like?

"You wouldn't believe me if I told you," she said to him.

"What?"

"That's what you said at the pool: *You wouldn't believe me if I told you.* What did you mean by that?"

Toby wasn't sure why, but he had the urge to throw caution to the wind and tell her everything. He wanted to tell someone because to keep this all to himself stressed him out. Yeah, Reggie could actually see the shadow, but Toby hadn't wanted to tell Reggie everything. Maybe it was time to get it all off his chest.

Staring down at her half sandwich, he started to tell Tabitha about *Hide-and-Seek*. How he cheated the game and broke it. How the shadow was now attached to him and he couldn't seem to get rid of it. For some reason, he felt she could handle the bizarre truth—that she wouldn't run off and tell someone he was crazy. It was somewhat liberating to finally unload the entirety of this crazy secret to someone else. He felt himself exhale in relief. Who knew keeping in such a secret was so exhausting?

"That sounds completely and utterly terrifying," she said, and looked behind him. "I can't see it."

Toby nodded. "I only see it in a mirror."

"For real?"

He nodded. "Yeah. You believe me?"

"It actually sounds too crazy to be made up. I know that you believe it and that's all that matters to me. People deal with their own darkness in different shapes and forms."

Okay, so she didn't completely believe him, but Toby understood. *He* couldn't even believe it, and he looked at it every day in the mirror. It was just a relief to get it all out and for her not to tell him he was crazy.

"And you thought you could drown it? How'd that work out for you?"

"I'm just trying everything I can. It didn't work, anyway."

"Have you told your mom or dad?"

"It's just my dad. Tried to tell him and my brother, but they didn't understand what I was talking about. They couldn't see it, either."

"But you've told me."

Toby sighed. "I don't know why."

She nodded. "Sometimes it's easier to tell a stranger. I get it. So why did you cheat the game?"

Toby picked at the sandwich. "Have you ever felt like you're never good at anything?"

"Well, yeah, you can't be good at everything."

"No," he stared at her. "Good at *anything at all.* Like a total loser."

She shook her head. "No, and you're not a loser."

His lips curved in a sarcastic smile. "Right. Have you not seen the way the teachers look at me? Like Dillonhall? I'm not worth their time."

"Look, life is what you make it. You can't think like that."

"I don't think like that. I *feel* it. It doesn't matter, anyway. I wanted to win, and I thought the only way I could was by cheating. It was stupid."

She didn't say anything to that and instead pulled a small, circular mirror from her bag. "Okay, let's see it."

Toby shook his head, scooting away from her. "No way."

She waved the mirror. "Come on, why not?"

"Because it's bad. *Really bad.* You don't even understand how bad."

She stared at him. "I can handle it."

He stared at her with wide eyes. "*I* can't even handle it."

"Okay, fine, you don't have to show me." She slipped the mirror back. "So, what are you going to do about it?"

Toby stared out at the soccer field, but he wasn't really seeing it. "I'm going to beat it. What other choice do I have?"

They sat a few minutes in silence before Tabitha said, "Let me see your phone."

He glanced at her. "Why?"

"Just let me see it," she said, annoyed.

Toby handed her his phone. She called a number, and her phone rang. Then she typed something into his phone and handed it back.

"I added myself as a contact. You know, if you ever need me to save you again."

Toby actually cracked a real smile. "Okay, thanks."

★ ★ ★

Toby went home after school. Usually, he was starving by the time he strolled into the kitchen, but today he felt different. Nervous, agitated, and he definitely had a serious loss of appetite. He grabbed a banana, when his phone alerted him with a text from Tabitha.

Hey, I know an excellent counselor you can talk to.
No way.
OK, fine.

Toby shook his head and clicked off the phone, but he couldn't help smiling a little. Tabitha was kinda cool. She took in everything he told her and didn't look at him weird. It was cool to have a new friend—not that he'd tell her that. Toby talked to a few kids at school, but he wouldn't call them friends. He used to have a best friend named Manny, but he moved away with his family when Toby was in middle school. Since then, Toby kind of shut himself off from other kids. Maybe it was time to open up again.

Just to keep up his energy, he attempted to eat the banana. He got about half of it down before he felt like gagging. His head jerked up when a knock sounded at the front door. Who could that be?

He answered the door to a clean-cut police officer with brown skin, short buzzed hair, and a mustache. Toby swallowed hard. He still had the half-eaten banana in his hand.

"I'm looking for Toby Billings," he said.

"Th–that's me." Toby adjusted the beanie on his head.

"I'm Officer Jimenez, Toby. I'm here about the break–in and vandalism at Freddy Fazbear's Pizza and Games. Dan Harbor stated that you work there, and that you were on shift that evening. He gave me your address."

"Uh–huh."

Officer Jimenez had a small notebook and pen in his hand. "Can you walk me through your shift that evening?"

Toby looked at his banana. "Well, um, I vacuumed the carpet in the main party room and arcade. Swept up in the bathrooms. Wiped down tables, put up chairs. Picked up trash from the floor. My regular stuff."

"What time did you end your shift? Mr. Harbor said you must have forgotten to write on your time sheet what time you left."

Toby scratched his neck with his free hand. "Um, yeah, I was off at 11:00 p.m. I must have forgotten to sign out." *Yeah, because I'd run out.*

Officer Jimenez wrote something down in the note-book. "What time did you last see the game before it was vandalized?"

"Um, well, after closing." *Wait, should I have said that?*

"So around 10:00 p.m.?"

He nodded. "Yep, I think so."

"There were no signs of a break–in, Toby. Did you

notice anyone hanging around who wasn't supposed to be there after closing?"

He blew out a breath, shook his head slowly. "Nope. No one. Same thing I told Dan. I checked the stalls and the play area where kids tend to hide."

Officer Jimenez looked directly into Toby's eyes. "Toby, I want you to be completely honest with me."

"Yeah, okay."

"Did you vandalize the game *Hide-and-Seek*?"

"What?"

"I have to ask. You were the last one to see the game. You were working in the restaurant near the time of the crime. Everyone else was in the kitchen. You didn't sign out at the end of your shift. Maybe you were in a hurry because you'd vandalized the game. Maybe you were upset with your boss or someone. I've seen it happen before. And you didn't want to get in trouble, so you ran. Is that how it happened?"

Toby stepped back. "*No*, it wasn't me." *Yes, it was.*

"Okay," he said sternly. "That's all for now. Let Mr. Harbor know if you remember anything else or if you want to tell him anything else."

"Yeah, okay."

Officer Jimenez gave a nod of his head. "Have a good day."

Toby nodded in return. He closed the door, still tense. He wondered if the officer believed him. It didn't sound like it. It sounded like he thought Toby did it. He wondered if he was going to get caught.

Toby scrubbed a hand down his face. He had too many things to focus on. He was trying his best to figure out how to be free of the shadow. He also had to worry if he was going to get caught for breaking *Hide-and-Seek*.

One thing at a time, please.

He walked into the kitchen and threw the half-eaten banana in the garbage, then detoured into the front room. Beside his dad's recliner was a small tray table with a lighter and an ashtray. He grabbed the lighter and flicked it, but it didn't light. He shook the lighter and flicked it again. This time, the flame lit.

He bit his bottom lip, staring at the small flame.

Maybe . . .

He released the igniter, then shook his head, muttering, "No freaking way." He tossed the lighter back on the tray.

"Was that a cop at the door?"

Toby jumped and whirled toward his dad. "Dad, you scared me! I didn't know you were home. Where's your car?"

"Getting a tune-up. I took the day off. Why the cop? What did he want with you?"

Toby cracked his knuckles. "Um, there was a break-in at Freddy's. Just a routine, questioning the employees who were there that night."

"Are you sure that's all it was?"

Toby blinked. "Yeah, why wouldn't I be?"

"You're not in any kind of trouble with breaking the law?"

"No, Dad." But he *was* in trouble.

Dad nodded, sat in his recliner, and turned on the television.

Toby walked away, then turned around to stare at his dad. He wanted to tell him the truth. He wanted to tell him that he cheated the game and destroyed it in anger. That the game had somehow attached to him and followed him home. He wanted to tell him so his dad could help him. So he could do what parents were supposed to do and help their kids when they were in trouble. Not just go through the motions of life like everything was okay when nothing was okay.

Not to pretend as if he never had a wife, and Toby and Connor never had a mom. Not to pretend as if he had two happy sons, who never called each other names or fought with their fists. As if life was all about working for a paycheck and watching sports.

"Dad?"

"Yeah, Tobes?" Dad said, not taking his eyes off the television.

"Why did Mom leave us?"

Dad didn't move his head from the screen. He didn't even flinch from the unexpected question. Toby wondered: When was the last time he ever saw his dad express any emotion, other than excitement or disgust from watching sports?

His dad was pretty much the mellow type. Toby had never seen him get seriously angry other than to yell at the refs on television. When he told Connor or Toby some-thing, it was all very calm and rational. Maybe it was a bonus to have a parent who didn't yell at you or scold you.

A minute passed as he waited for an answer from his dad, then two minutes. After five minutes, he realized he wasn't going to get an answer. He didn't know if it was because his dad didn't have one or if he didn't feel Toby could handle the truth.

Toby left the room to get ready for work.

Toby kept up with his regular routine and went in an hour before his shift to play games in the arcade. When he arrived, he noticed the *Hide-and-Seek* door propped open with a sign that stated, OUT OF ORDER.

Curious about *Hide-and-Seek*, he slid his hands inside his pockets and walked inside the game room. There was a tall, skinny guy standing by the control box. He had a laptop in his arms and seemed to be rebooting the game. His hair was blond and spiky, and he wore thick-framed glasses.

"Hey," Toby said to the guy. "How's it going?"

"All right," he said, eyeing him. "You know the game's out of order. You supposed to be in here?"

Toby cleared his throat. "Yeah, well, I work here. Gonna start my shift soon."

The tech guy seemed to relax a little. "Well, truthfully, then, I'm not doing so good. *Hide-and-Seek* here won't reboot. It says it's rebooting, but once it starts again, it goes back to the previous game every time. Must be some kind of wiring issue."

"It's stuck?"

"Yeah, stuck in game mode with the last player . . . uh, some kid named Toby."

All the blood seemed to rush out of Toby's head. He felt faint. "Really? Can't you just shut it down and restart it?"

"Normally, yeah. But something's off, I'm telling you. It won't stop the game. Never seen anything like it. Must be defunct. Dan ain't going to like to hear that. Not after he found out whoever tore up the game also took the rabbit."

"What?"

"Bonnie the Rabbit. The character. The black cutout rabbit for the game is gone. Whoever messed up the game took the rabbit right off the wall like some kind of souvenir. I can't believe it. Probably stuck it in their room or threw darts at it or something. Kids these days. No offense."

"Yeah. None taken."

The tech guy shut his laptop. "Well, going to go give Dan more bad news. I advised him to put in a camera from the beginning, but he was already dishing out a boatload for this game. Anyway, I'd stay clear of him today if I were you, kid. Maybe he shouldn't have ever installed this game."

"Yeah."

"Anyway, Dan's a good guy. He just wanted the best for the business. Give the families some entertainment, a place to have fun. But this is how he's repaid. Sucks, you know?"

When the tech guy left, Toby quickly strode through the kitchen, smelling pepperoni and melted cheese. He walked to the single employee bathroom and closed and locked the door behind him. He leaned his hands on either side of the pedestal sink, staring into the small mirror on the wall.

He stared into the darkness at his back, with all the anger and frustration he had inside of him. He hadn't taken the rabbit cutout from the game. No, it had decided all on its own to leave with Toby.

And as Toby stared hard at the shadow, two eyes opened and blinked at him.

Toby lurched back and yelped. His heart pounded like a drum.

He grabbed at the door, trying to open it, but because he was staring at the horror in the mirror, he forgot he'd locked it. He took his eyes off the shadow for a second, unlocked the handle, and whipped open the door. He rushed out and ran into Dan.

Toby stopped short, breathing hard. "Uh, Dan."

Dan gave him a weird look. "You all right, kid?"

Toby cracked his knuckles, trying not to shake in front of his boss. "Yeah, why?"

"You look nervous about something."

Toby adjusted his beanie. "Um, no, I'm fine. Really." His face heated because he was so far from fine.

Dan eyed him some more. "Okay, kid. Whatever you say." Then he walked into his office.

Toby sagged against the bathroom door. His phone signaled with a new text. It was Tabitha again.

What about an herbalist? They can give you stuff to calm your nerves.
No way.
Well, it was just an idea. I'm here at Freddy's. Come meet me in the arcade.

Surprised, Toby clicked off his phone as he hurried to the arcade to find Tabitha, who was peering over a kid's shoulder as he played a game. Reggie was right beside her, eating pink cotton candy on a stick.

Toby stopped at her side, rubbing his damp palms on the shirt. "What are you doing here?" He was already nervous, and it made him even more nervous to have her at the scene of the crime that he had confessed to her. When he'd told her his secrets, she'd been someone separate from his everyday life. She didn't know much about him or Freddy's, but now that his separate worlds were colliding, it felt weird and uncomfortable.

Tabitha smiled as she looked around the arcade. "This is a cool place. I've never actually been here. My parents aren't into places like these."

"It's a family pizza restaurant."

She shrugged. "They're vegans." She looked back to Toby, her smile dropping away. "Hey, are you okay?"

"Yeah, fine."

"Who's your friend, Toby?" Reggie butted in. "Hey, I'm Reggie."

Tabitha glanced at Reggie. "Tabitha."

Reggie looked at Toby and lifted his eyebrows a couple of times in an annoying way. "You come here often?" he asked her.

"No, first time."

Toby frowned at Reggie. He knew Tabitha wasn't a regular. What was up with him? He took Tabitha by the elbow and guided her away. Over her shoulder, he watched Reggie keep pointing to Toby, then to his own back. Then he made a big gesture like he was huge, then a scary face. Then he mouthed very slowly, *Shadow. Bigger.*

Toby rolled his eyes, then asked Tabitha, "What are you doing here?"

"I want to see the game."

Toby shook his head. "No way. Can't. It's out of order. No one is supposed to be in there."

"Can I at least see the outside of it? Please, I'm curious."

Toby sighed. He didn't think it was such a good idea, but he felt if he didn't let her see it, she'd just keep on about it until she got her way.

"Fine, but then you better go."

"Okay."

"And look, I trusted you with this. Don't make me regret it."

"You won't. I promise." She crossed her heart with her finger.

Toby led her out of the arcade and to the door of *Hide-and-Seek*. He crossed his arms as she studied the shadowed rabbit and the logo.

"Seems so innocent, but then you know it's something dark and scary to a friend." She looked at Toby. "How do you feel?"

"Like it's always there and I'm never going to get rid of it." Toby shifted uncomfortably. Why was he always telling her stuff like that?

"You'll beat this, Toby. I'm making a list of ideas, like the ones I've been texting you about. I'm going to help you figure out how to solve this. We're going to get you in a better place."

Toby just stared at her, not knowing what to say. Other than *why?* Why did she want to help him? Why did she even care? He wasn't sure he wanted her help, anyway. He wasn't sure he could totally trust someone in that way. It had been so long since he trusted anyone . . . he'd learned being let down pretty much sucked.

He adjusted his beanie and sighed. "Whatever you want to do."

Toby was running from someone. Or something. He was in a park at night. The pale light of the full moon washed across the scene. Stars twinkled above. Trees and bushes loomed across the area surrounding a small playground. His heartbeats were running a mile a minute. His breaths were coming out of his mouth at a pace he was certain he couldn't maintain. He hid behind a tree, trying to catch his breath. Something dark and fast torpedoed past him—so fast, Toby's hair moved as if brushed by the wind.

"Holy cow," Toby whispered. It was the shadow, but somehow it moved faster than his eyes could follow. How was he going to escape something so quick?

He launched himself off the tree, running by a grocery store and a school. The streets were empty of cars and people. He spotted a police station up ahead. Had to get there and get help.

He shoved through the doors. "Someone help me! There's something after me! Please!"

But when he looked around, there were no officers.

"Hello? Where is everyone? Come on, I need help here!"

But the place was deserted, as if everyone had just walked away at the same time.

Toby jerked his head toward the doorway. He felt the darkness coming. He wasn't sure how, but he knew it was getting closer.

He whipped his head to the left and to the right, his nerves scrambling throughout his body. He spotted an empty desk and dove behind it, squatting underneath it, pulling his knees to his chin. He heard the doors to the police station burst open. Toby started at the sound and squeezed his eyes shut.

Please don't find me. Please don't find me.

The shadow raced past the desk. Toby heard the *clank* of the jail cell doors. Finding it empty, the darkness roared at him with the timbre of a thousand angry beasts. Monstrous. Terrifying. Toby bit his bottom lip in order not to scream himself. His entire body started to shake.

The shadow rushed by the desk again, and Toby sat for a moment, waiting to get some distance between him and the shadow. He licked his dry lips. *I think it's gone.*

He slowly crawled out from his hiding place, but when he stood, he froze in horror.

The shadow reared itself before him, its darkness crackling with energy. The shadow's narrowed eyes peered down at Toby.

Toby stepped back, and the shadow moved closer.

"Stay away from me!" Toby shouted.

But the shadow continued to lurch closer. The nearer it got, the bigger it became, until it loomed over Toby like a mountain of unforgiving darkness. The shadow's power had created a vortex of energy that blew through the room. Toby's hair flew back, and his clothes flattened against his body.

Toby threw his hands over his head as the darkness crashed down, swallowing and surrounding him. Anger, despair, fear seemed to fill him up. He swung out with fists in terror and rage, trying to fight it, but his arms just swung through air.

The shadow devoured him: It leached into his eyes and through his nostrils. Toby shrieked—swallowing the darkness down his throat.

Toby woke up screaming. "No!"

He jumped out of bed, fell to the floor. Darkness was all around him. He launched himself backward, his entire body shaking. He hit a cold wall, and he realized he was home in his room. It wasn't real. Just a nightmare. But it had seemed *so real.*

It was one of the worst nightmares of his life.

His eyes stung, and he started to cry, his shoulders shaking. Because if he'd learned one thing from the nightmare, it was that the shadow was so much stronger than him. And that it wanted to win at all costs.

He wiped at his leaky nose and howled in frustration. He hated this. He hated the shadow. He wanted it gone. He reached for his back, clawed at it. "Get. Off. Of. Me." He scratched. He scraped. "Leave me alone!"

He tore off his shirt and dug into his skin as if he could tear the shadow away. He clawed and slashed with his own hands. Digging into his skin. "I want you gone!"

He felt the burn of the scratches, the drips of blood.

"Just leave me alone!" he screamed, and cried some more, curling into a ball on the floor.

But he knew the shadow was still there. That it wouldn't leave.

He could sense it as if it were a part of him now.

★ ★ ★

"Dude, Tobes, what is up with you lately?" Connor asked when Toby walked into the kitchen. Connor stood at the kitchen counter, eating two breakfast sandwiches. He looked at Toby with wide eyes as if seeing him in a way he'd never seen him before. "Are you still sick? Maybe we should get Dad to take you to the doctor or something."

"Just leave me alone, Connor." There was no way Connor could handle what was really wrong with him.

"Tobes, I'm serious. You need help. I can tell something's wrong with you. You walk around like a freaking zombie. You're barely eating, and you're not your whiny self. It's weird, and you're already weird. So, that makes you weirder than usual."

"Shut up." Toby made a face and shook his head. "Don't act like you care."

Connor beat his chest with his sandwich. "What? What do you mean? I care."

"Whatever. You only care about yourself and how you think you're the best at everything."

"That's not true. And just because I'm good at stuff, a lot of stuff, you don't have to get all bent about it."

Toby gave a small laugh. "Every day of your life, you tell me how you're the best and I'm nothing. That I'm a loser."

Connor didn't have much to say to that, so he just said, "Okay, well, I'm pretty close to being the best."

Toby's eyes widened. "*No, you're not, Connor.* You're not

the best, and I'm not the best. You only think you are because, for some reason, you and Dad think you're so great. So pathetic, is more like it."

Connor rolled his eyes. "This is about Dad, isn't it? You're jealous."

Toby jerked back. "What?"

"You're jealous because Dad and I spend a lot of time watching sports. Dad always invites you to watch with us, you know that. Why don't you hang out with us instead of barricading yourself in your room?"

Toby swallowed hard. "You don't even know what you're talking about. So stop."

"Whatever, Tobes, you know it's true. But I'm not going to argue with you when you're practically ready to keel over at any minute."

"Do you even know how stupid you always sound about being the best at everything? There has to be someone out there better than you. You know that, right?"

Connor shrugged a shoulder. "Whatever, Tobes. Listen, I told you, I'm not going to—"

"*You listen.*" Toby pointed a finger at Connor, ticked off and tired of all the dumb things that came out of his mouth. "Just so you know, there's a new game at Freddy's and I'm playing it right now, and *I'm winning.*" Yeah, it was a half-truth. Toby was still playing this hide-and-seek game with the shadow. He'd just taken the game home with him. He was pretty sure the rabbit was definitely winning, though. But Connor didn't have to know that.

Connor tossed his sandwich on his plate and crossed his arms. "Oh, the truth finally comes out. There's a new game at Freddy's, and you didn't even want to tell me so that you could try and beat me at something. News flash, little brother: It doesn't count until I've played. And once I do, I'll beat it and take my rightful spot at the top."

Toby smiled as an idea dawned on him. "Sure."

Connor saw his smile and frowned. "Sure, what?"

"Sure, you'll beat me." Toby walked out of the kitchen and down the hallway.

"Of course I will, little brother." Connor followed him. He always had to get the last word. "That's the reality."

Toby walked into the bathroom. He turned toward his brother, crossed his arms.

Connor stood outside the door. "So, what's the game called?"

"*Hide-and-Seek.*"

"Perfect. Sounds like a kid's game, so it'll be easy. I'll go there after work tonight and snag the top spot. Not a problem."

"No, you won't," Toby told him.

Connor just stared at Toby. "Why not?"

Toby nodded toward the mirror, finally wanting his brother to see the truth. To see this awful shadow that wouldn't leave him alone. Toby had been the ultimate player by battling the shadow, and he wanted Connor to finally know.

He looked back at Connor. "Because *I'm* still playing and *I'm* going to win it if it's the last thing I do." He pointed his finger at Connor. "I'm going to beat you, Connor. You just wait and see. I'll be the winner and you'll be the freaking loser! It's going to be the best day of my life! Do you hear me? Best. Day. Of. My. Life!"

Connor didn't look at the mirror. He just stared at Toby with wide eyes. "I see." Then he simply shook his head and raised his hands as if surrendering. "You know what, Tobes. Fine. Go ahead. Beat me. I want you to."

Toby's mouth dropped open. "Wh-what?"

"I give up being the best. It's getting old, fighting with you all the time. I mean, dude, have you looked at yourself lately? Really looked at yourself in the mirror? You look sick and exhausted and you're still fighting with me, like it's all that matters in the world instead of your health. This whole competition thing has gotten way out of hand, and it's time to stop. So, if it takes you winning and me losing, then I'm done."

Toby didn't know what to say.

"Anyway, I got to get to work. If you need to stay home, do it. I'll tell Dad you were really sick. Just get some rest, little brother." Connor turned away.

Toby watched Connor walk down the hallway and disappear, then heard the front door shut. Connor didn't care to be the best anymore. After all the games, all the competitions, all the fighting for years . . . and he had practically conceded to Toby. In a daze, Toby turned toward the bathroom mirror.

Toby stared at himself in the mirror. Really stared at himself. His skin was paler than he'd ever seen it. His cheeks were sunken in. His eyes looked like dark pits in his face. He finally moved his gaze to the shadow.

Clawing and scratching at his skin must have really ticked it off. Not only had it grown in size, but its eyes stared at him with a chilling glare. Then something moved within its face, and that's when he noticed the shadow had formed a mouth.

A row of spiked teeth flashed into a smile.

Toby's eyes widened in shock, and he started to pant in short breaths. The shadow radiated fear and anger, and just like in his dream, the shadow loomed behind him, a predator waiting to strike.

Toby felt the urge to cower into a ball on the floor. The shadow was too powerful. Too strong. And Toby knew he was too tired and too weak to fight it anymore.

"Why are you doing this to me?" he yelled at the mirror. "I just want this done! Over!"

Exhausted, Toby leaned his elbows on the bathroom counter, placing his face in his hands. Silent tears streamed down his cheeks. He finally accepted that he was never going to be rid of the shadow. It was going to stay attached to him forever. He'd tried everything he could think of to get it off. Nothing seemed to hurt the darkness. The more he tried, the bigger, stronger, and more horrifying it became, and the worse it made him feel.

Maybe the shadow had attached to him so easily because he'd been in a bad place emotionally. He'd been wrapped up in some crazy competition with his brother all these years. Nothing Connor or anyone did had made him a loser. It had been his own sense of competition and messed-up beliefs. True, jealousy of Connor and Dad's relationship had made him think of himself as an outcast, like he didn't belong even in his own home. But if he was being honest, *he* was the one who had slowly separated himself further and further from his dad and brother because he wanted to win. All these years, he wanted to be a winner just like Connor. But none of that seemed to matter compared to the torture he'd endured with the shadow for the past few days.

He raised his gaze to the shadow's and took a cue from his brother. "Okay," he said. "You win. You beat me. I give up. Whatever. I don't care anymore."

At that moment, Toby blinked as he felt the heaviness of his back lighten. Surprised, he slowly stood up straight in front of the mirror. The shadow was still there, but it had gone back to the size of when he'd first seen it in his bedroom. The eyes and mouth had disappeared into the darkness. All he felt was a little tickle in the middle of his back once again.

With that realization, it was like something clicked inside of him. A veil had lifted, and he saw everything with sudden clarity.

Just like Toby, the shadow had only wanted to win.

Toby walked out of the bathroom to change, and his cell phone rang. He looked at the screen and read Tabitha's name before answering. "Hello?"

"Hey, how are you? Do you need any more saving yet?" she asked.

"Nope."

"Meet me before school behind the bleachers. I have some more ideas to run by you about the shadow."

"No, I'm not going to school today."

"Why? What's happened?"

Toby rubbed his face. "Look, I'm ready to end this once and for all. It's time."

"What do you mean, Toby?"

"Just don't worry about it. I know what I have to do now."

"What? What do you have to do? Does it involve reiki healing? 'Cause that's at the top of my list."

"What?" Toby shook his head. "No. Gotta go, Tab. If I forget to tell you, you're a good friend. I'll see you tomorrow."

"Wait!"

Toby clicked off the call, then turned off his phone. It was time to go back to Freddy Fazbear's Pizza and Games. It was time to finish *Hide-and-Seek*.

Toby walked into Freddy Fazbear's Pizza and Games with a cool determination. A deadly calm had come over him. He finally knew what he had to do to finish this. It had come to him suddenly. How he cheated *Hide-and-Seek* and then the shadow rabbit had followed him home. How the technician said the game was still in play. It wouldn't reboot because Toby had to finish the game. The darkness had wanted him to concede because Toby had cheated. It was all clear to him now. He'd been so fixated on the fact that the shadow was on him that he hadn't focused on the end game. This wasn't like *Ultimate Battle Warrior,* where you beat each other senseless. This was a strategy game.

The toughest one he had ever played in his life.

He walked into the restaurant, and there were only a few little kids playing in the play area and arcade since it was a school day. He walked through the arcade, and of course, Reggie was there. Toby realized Reggie was always there, and he wondered if the kid even had a home.

This time Reggie just stared behind Toby, as if he couldn't take his eyes off the shadow.

"Guess, uh, you never got rid of the shadow," Reggie said. "At least it's small again. Dude, last time I saw you, it was massive."

"I have to complete the *Hide-and-Seek* game."

Reggie blinked. "I thought it was broken."

"It's in play, and I'm going to finish it."

"That's the game that started all of this? But how are you gonna do that when it's all busted up?"

"I'll figure it out."

Reggie nodded and held out his fist. "Respect, dude. The fire's back within you. Do what you gotta do."

Toby tapped his fist to Reggie's and walked passed him.

"Hey," Reggie said, and Toby turned back around.

"Can I have that girl Tabitha's digits?"

Toby just shook his head and made his way to the game, stopping at the door of *Hide-and-Seek*. The OUT OF ORDER sign was still taped to the door. It was locked, so Toby put in coins to open it and entered the room.

There were fresh white patches on the wall, where Toby had busted open a few holes. All the broken pieces were gone off the floor. The small barricade was completely torn down. There were no new cutouts on the wall. The pegs were still bare.

Taking a breath, Toby went to the control box and turned on the power. Instrumental music blared through the speakers. After it completely booted up, Toby saw his name still in play.

Toby dug out a peppermint toothpick from his pocket and slipped it into his mouth. He adjusted the beanie on his head.

A voice bellowed from the speakers, *"Are you ready to continue? Or do you forfeit the game?"*

Toby's finger hovered over the "Forfeit" button. Once he pushed the bottom, he knew everything would go back to normal. The shadow would be gone, and the rabbit would return to *Hide-and-Seek*. He could go back to his life of being in control of his own body.

And he'd be free.

Toby bit his bottom lip as a familiar feeling spread over him. You see, he couldn't really get over the fact that the shadow had attached to him. That the shadow had played the ultimate cheat on Toby by making him hurt himself. By making him believe he was going crazy just so it could win the freaking game.

The shadow had wanted to win.

And Toby had let it.

Toby shut his eyes, trembling with anger. "You thought you could beat me," he said. "You thought you could turn my own cheating back on me. Well, I got a surprise for you. I'm not a loser. *You're the loser.*" He opened his eyes, punched down on the "Continue" button with heated determination, then turned his back to the park wall. He felt the shadow's anger slam over him.

Jaw tight, Toby rushed backward toward the pegs where the tree was supposed to hang, and rammed himself onto the sticks. The pegs stabbed through his back. Toby's body stiffened as he gasped. His toothpick dropped from his mouth. He felt the shadow release. The dark energy faded away from him as if it never existed.

"I won," he whispered as blood dripped from his mouth. He smiled right before his eyes gently closed.

The instrumental music restarted through the speakers.

"Welcome to Hide-and-Seek! Enter your name to try to find Bonnie, and let's begin!"

ABOUT THE AUTHORS

Scott Cawthon is the author of the bestselling video game series *Five Nights at Freddy's*, and while he is a game designer by trade, he is first and foremost a storyteller at heart. He is a graduate of The Art Institute of Houston and lives in Texas with his family.

Andrea Rains Waggener is an author, novelist, ghostwriter, essayist, short story writer, screenwriter, copywriter, editor, poet, and a proud member of Kevin Anderson & Associates' team of writers. In a past she prefers not to remember much, she was a claims adjuster, JCPenney's catalog order taker (before computers!), appellate court clerk, legal writing instructor, and lawyer. Writing in genres that vary from her chick-lit novel, *Alternate Beauty*, to her dog how-to book, *Dog Parenting*, to her self-help book, *Healthy, Wealthy, and Wise*, to ghostwritten memoirs to ghostwritten YA, horror, mystery, and mainstream fiction projects, Andrea still manages to find time to watch the rain and obsess over her dog and her knitting, art, and music projects. She lives with her husband and said dog on the Washington coast, and if she isn't at home creating something, she can be found walking on the beach.

Kelly Parra is the author of YA novels *Graffiti Girl, Invisible Touch*, and other supernatural short stories. In addition to her independent works, Kelly works with Kevin Anderson & Associates on a variety of projects. She resides in Central Coast, California, with her husband and two children.

Larson pulled his brown sedan just inside the gaping doorway of the abandoned factory. He turned off the engine and looked around. A murky twilight was beginning to slip down the mountains on the far side of the lake, threatening to swallow the remainder of the day's light. Larson figured it would be dark in about an hour. Looking in the rearview mirror, he noticed a couple security lights mounted on tall poles, standing like sentinels guarding the factory and the dock extending out into the lake beyond. Some of that light would make it in through this door, he figured. And he'd need the light if he didn't start moving.

"Get on with it," Larson commanded himself.

Picking up his portable radio and tucking it in his jacket pocket, he reached for the plastic garbage bag into which he'd stuffed the evidence he'd purloined from the evidence locker. It had taken some fast talking to get it past the sergeant on duty. He couldn't explain what he needed the evidence for because he hadn't quite convinced himself that he actually needed it. His intuition said he did. His logical mind was laughing hysterically.

Getting out of the sedan, holding the garbage bag, Larson looked around again. He waited and listened. Unless a situation was pressing, he always liked to take a minute to assess where he was. Take it in. Feel it.

It wasn't going to require a minute to assess this place. In just five seconds, Larson had felt enough. What he felt was so strong it hit him like an invisible force, and he had to grab the open sedan door to steady himself. Larson wasn't sure he believed in evil, but if evil did exist, he'd have said it resided here, or at least it was visiting.

He cocked his head and listened for another few seconds. He heard nothing but the sound of cars passing on the street beyond the building and a couple crows cawing from atop a corroded shed about ten feet from the factory's outer walls.

Wait. Was that movement he'd seen? He turned to look at a yellowed, dirty window in the shed. No. Nothing was there.

Larson quietly closed the sedan's door. The space he was in looked big enough for two more cars like his, and beyond it, another larger room beckoned.

It was dim inside the old factory, but Larson could see well enough. He could hear, too, and what he heard told him where he needed to go.

From the far side of the expanse that opened up ahead of him, scraping and rustling sounds warred with *plinks*, *thuds*, and *clatters*. Someone was in there.

Larson stopped and wrapped the plastic bag's ties around his wrist. Once it was secured, he drew his gun. Extending the automatic in front of him, he crept forward.

A whisper came from what felt like a few feet away, just up ahead. Larson went rigid. Someone was close enough that he could hear them whisper? Why couldn't he see them?

He took a breath, steadied himself, then strode to the edge of a huge room dominated by a massive blue trash compactor. The compactor contained a pile of electronic and metal debris.

And next to the compactor's chute, his quarry stood.

"A strange cloaked figure," Larson muttered. Yep, there it was.

Larson pivoted left and right, trying to find the source of the whisper. But he was alone on a wide concrete platform that encircled the factory floor.

Alone, with the strange cloaked figure.

The figure didn't seem to care about Larson's presence, though. It looked to be sorting trash. It was emptying a large garbage bag. Larson watched gears, hinges, and tangles of wire drop from the bag. Then he saw the bag let go of the distorted face of a fox wearing a pirate's eye patch. The disconnected arms of a fox followed, one arm ending in a hook.

Foxy. Larson recognized the animatronic from Freddy's. He was on the right track.

The broken Foxy and what looked like other robotic debris slid down the compactor chute into the square belly of the steel beast. When the remains hit the sides of the compactor, the *clang* brought Larson to his senses.

"Stop!" he shouted at the figure.

The figure turned and took a step toward Larson. Larson raised his gun and squared his stance.

"Leave him alone," Jake said to Andrew.

Jake had no sense of himself as an individual body now, but he could still act like one when he tried really hard. Like now.

He threw his nonexistent shoulder into Andrew's equally nonexistent chest, and the two of them began fighting for control over the animatronic container that held them. The animatronic lurched back and forth in what Jake was sure must have looked like a spastic dance to the detective who was pointing his gun.

"Let me take care of him!" Andrew shouted. "I can . . . stop . . . him." His choppy words reflected the effort he was expending trying to wrest control of the animatronic from Jake. Andrew had already proven he could command it at least a little, because Jake hadn't taken the step toward the cop.

"But you'll hurt him," Jake reminded Andrew, shoving harder with his imaginary shoulder.

Andrew grunted, then said, panting, "We have to get rid of this stuff or it will hurt more people."

Jake concentrated and raised his imaginary hand. "Yes, but not by killing someone else." Frowning and throwing every bit of his will into what he wanted to do, Jake was able to overcome Andrew. The animatronic's skeletal hand came up and slapped the compactor's start button. Then Jake took a solid grip on Andrew and prepared to do what had to be done.

Larson flinched when the compactor started. The sudden bass rumble and reverberation momentarily stupefied him. Then, in the quarter second he spent to process that, he got his next shock.

The figure threw itself into the chute.

From where he stood on the upper platform of the big room, Larson was able to see the endoskeleton of the figure land in the spinning, thrashing heap of metal. Immediately, the parts started to consume the figure as everything churned inside the compactor. A metal press began shoving its way into the writhing mass of junk.

Larson started to run toward the chute, but the press plowed through the junk faster than he could cover the yards between him and the switch. It moved steadily, inexorably through the twisted mound with a roaring screech that sounded like a clash between a behemoth and defenseless creatures wailing in their death throes. It looked that way, too. So much of the junk in the pile were parts of robotic toys and animatronics that it was easy to humanize the pile and see it as a mass grave being defiled by the powerful metallic arm of a monster. All Larson could do was stand and watch the compactor destroy the parts that had made up the cloaked figure and everything it had been collecting.

As soon as Jake and Andrew landed in the compacting junk, the baseball field returned to Jake's consciousness. He heard his dad laugh, and he tasted a fresh peanut . . . and he felt himself begin to float free again.

Jake resisted, focusing intensely on the junk surrounding him. He couldn't leave Andrew!

The memory was so strong, though. Even as he put all his attention on the junk, his dad's face and the warm sun buoyed him.

"Andrew, grab my hand!" he shouted.

Andrew reached up. As soon as he did, he, too, began to disconnect from the endoskeleton.

Jake was so relieved, so thrilled, that he let the memory embrace him again. He and Andrew both began to move away from their physical confines, as if they were being carried by a sleek, swift sailboat toward that wonderful sunny day in the baseball field . . . but only for a few seconds.

Then Andrew was tugged downward. He was being yanked toward the infected robotic parts below.

"No!" Jake shouted. He tried to hang on to Andrew, but the force resisting him was so strong!

Jake looked down. Below him, a bizarre presence of color and movement was brawling with everything in the compactor, including the animatronic Jake and Andrew were in. This chaotic collection of muddy brown, dirty yellow, and shocking red pulsed with rage.

"Come on, Andrew!" Jake called.

"I'm trying! But I can't! Something's got me!" Andrew called back.

Jake felt like he and Andrew were being stretched between two forces. From somewhere beyond this dirty factory, the good feelings of Jake's memory boosted them. From below, density roiled around Andrew, keeping them anchored. Jake thought the density was Andrew's pain.

Then he realized he was wrong. It had nothing to do with Andrew!

"Andrew," Jake said. "There's something else in here with us."

"It's him!" Andrew cried out. He sounded terrified.

Jake focused harder on his memory: He ate a hot, salty peanut, and he looked into his dad's warm, happy gaze.

Larson couldn't move. He was mesmerized by the compacting junk . . . and by the inexplicable light rising from it. What was that?

He realized he was still aiming at the crumpling, deconstructing Stitchwraith and holstered his gun. He rubbed his eyes. Was he seeing things? It looked like a faint aurora borealis was rising up from the convulsing junk.

"Yes!" Jake cried.

Andrew was breaking loose!

Then, out of the nearly fully compressed junk, the contorted but identifiable shape of what looked like a burned skeletal man thrust upward. With ashy, see-through skin that revealed dried-up but still quivering organs, the man-thing looked like a creature from hell. Its limbs broken and bursting through the cracked skin, its face misshapen, its torso twisted—the creature took shape while Jake watched.

When Jake saw the man's bones crack, fold, and reshape into what appeared to be rabbit ears, he yelled, "Andrew, come on!" Rabbit ears unfolded from the back of the creature's skull and stretched upright, and the creature heaved itself toward Andrew. Jake had hold of Andrew, and he was sure all but just the tiniest amount of Andrew's essence was in his grasp. But the creature was trying to keep hold of his friend.

"No!" Jake shouted.

Jake focused again on his good memory, but this time, it didn't loosen Andrew anymore. It just started taking Jake away from Andrew.

Jake couldn't let that happen—he wasn't going to allow Andrew to be hurt anymore. Jake had to stay and fight!

Blocking out anything good he'd ever felt, Jake anchored

himself back into the animatronic. He faced the enemy in the compactor.

As soon as Jake released his memory, the creature shifted its attention to Jake. Jake felt the creature claw at him. It felt like he was being mauled and pummeled by a force filled with a never-ending need to inflict pain.

But he didn't give in to it. Throwing everything he had into his effort and drawing on the power of his memory, Jake turned himself into a massive bat of intention, and he swung away, knocking Andrew loose from the evil that held him.

Andrew, suddenly free, was sucked away; and he vanished.

Jake, however, couldn't untangle himself from the relentless rabbit creature. He fell back into the seething junk and was engulfed in blackness.

The trash compactor opened, and Larson watched it tip upward and disgorge its flattened mass of broken animatronic and robotic pieces. From above the compactor, what looked like a dying ember fizzled and fell back into the compressed junk.

"What just happened?" Larson asked the room.

It didn't answer.

Larson shook his head and looked around. His gaze landed on a pot with two red flowers shaped like starfish. It sat at a tilt against the upper lip of the compactor, unaffected by the pressure that had just smashed through the rest of the bizarre debris the figure had collected.

Larson thought about going down the stairs to poke around the compressed junk, but he didn't see the point. Whether he was right or wrong about what had just happened, it was done. So he turned and headed back to his sedan.

There, he dropped the trash bag he'd carried inside onto the floor next to the sedan. He wasn't sure what to do with it. He'd planned on using it as a way to communicate to the Stitchwraith, but now . . .

He leaned into his sedan and pulled out a mini tape recorder.

"The, ah, Stitchwraith appears to be dead," he said into the recorder. He felt like an idiot. *Dead* wasn't the right word for what he'd just witnessed, was it?

And what exactly did he see? He took a breath and spoke into the recorder. "I saw an animatronic endoskeleton with a doll's head and some kind of battery, wearing a hooded trench coat putting stuff in a trash compactor and pulverizing it. It also destroyed itself. I think the stuff in the compactor came from the Fazbear Entertainment Distribution Center and also from the site where the serial killer William Afton, the one notorious for wearing a rabbit costume, died." He stopped the recorder and thought for a second.

Oh, what the hell. He started recording again. "I don't believe in ghosts, but after what I just saw, I'm not so sure about anything anymore. I mean, from where I stood, I swore it looked like the Stitchwraith was an animatronic contraption—and there was some kind of supernatural light coming out of it. Like, a ghost? Like the animatronic was haunted by ghosts. Maybe the ghosts were kids Afton killed? Or maybe it was Afton himself." He stopped the recording and sighed.

Who was going to believe any of this?

Tossing the recorder in his sedan, Larson turned his back to the inner part of the factory and looked out through the exterior opening to the lake. The sky above the mountains was tinged with the faintest hint of pink.

Maybe he should take Ryan hiking the next time he got to spend time with his son.

Behind the unsuspecting Larson, the compacted trash began to move. Making a quiet rustling sound Larson didn't hear, the junk rose from the trash compactor and began to arrange itself into an upright being.

As it began to assemble itself, the being sucked in all the remaining junk and debris in the factory. However, it also rejected some of the waste. Just as it started to form, the vaguely man-shaped structure of trash shuddered for a second, and then it ejected part of itself. A mutilated mass of robotic endoskeleton and crumpled fabric spewed through the air and landed several feet away. When the rejected detritus hit the concrete, it lay still.

The rest of the trash from the compactor continued its transfiguration.

It formed itself out of animatronic body parts, but not in

any logical way. They were joining all haywire. Heads were being used as joints, arms as legs, and legs as arms. A torso formed from the hips and chest and belly of three animatronics, but each part was put in the wrong place. Hands were inserted at random all over the structure. Woven through all these misplaced pieces were wires and gears, which created a labyrinthine circulatory system connecting hinges to gears and screws and nails to eyes and noses and mouths.

With each additional piece clamping into place, the miscreation stood taller and taller until it was nearly fifteen feet tall. Then, looming over the detective, it leaned to the side and lifted a macabre head up to a neck made from shins.

The head, like the rest of the being, was made from animatronic parts—fingers, toes, wires, hinges. Within those parts, two gaping black holes looked out at the world with pure malevolence. And from the top of the unnatural structure, what looked like two rabbit ears made of even more animatronic parts unfolded and canted forward. They were aimed right at the detective.